CYDONIA

6

ESCAPE OR BE EATEN

MATT SYLVESTER

PUBLISHED BY: Matt Sylvester

Copyright © 2018

ISBN: 978-1-7322019-1-0

CYDONIA 6—DIAGRAM

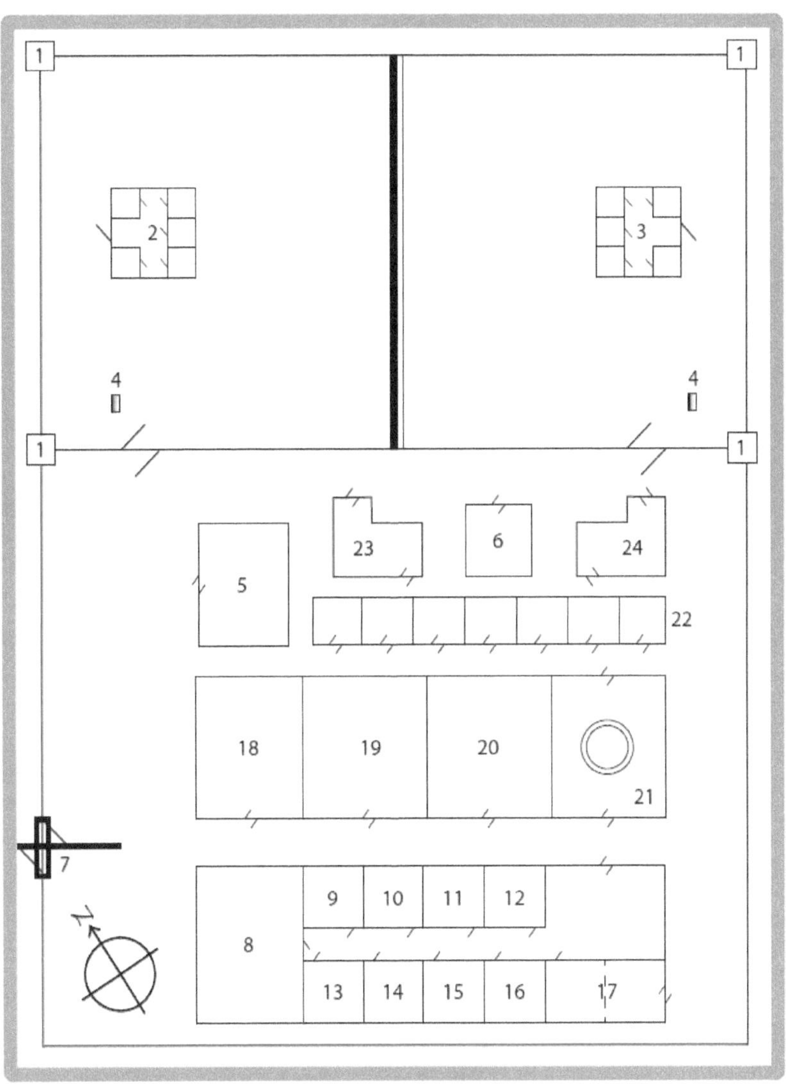

CYDONIA 6—LEGEND

1	Guard Towers	10	Dr. Selleck's Bunk	19	Barracks 1 (inactive)
2	Male Inmate Barracks	11	Doctor's Office	20	Barracks 2 (inactive)
3	Female Inmate Barracks	12	Storage Room A	21	Communications
4	Isolation Hole	13	Hilda's Bunk	22	Barracks 3 (inactive)
5	Inmate Kitchen	14	Headmaster's Bunk	23	Male Latrine (inactive)
6	Marriage Hut	15	Headmaster's Office	24	Female Latrine (inactive)
7	Main Gate	16	Storage Room B		Gravel Road
8	Classroom	17	Staff Kitchen & Lounge		Lines of Division
9	Edgar's Bunk	18	Waterworks & Furnace		South Fence Gates
					Satellite Dish

CHAPTER 1

The day's third feeding began just like the two that preceded it and the one that followed. Edgar, the brutish male enforcer who specialized in bullying, beatings, and force-feeding, exited his bunk and walked across the administration area to the inmates' kitchen, where he filled ten steel pots with water and set each of them on burners.

The five pots designated for the male inmates were marked with black, hand-painted numbers ranging sequentially from 20 to 24. The five pots allocated to the female inmates were also numbered 20 to 24, but the digits were painted in white. Every day, the numbered pots were set on the same burners, in the same order, and filled with the same amount of water. Cross-contamination of assigned foods had to be avoided at all costs; so, like the inmates, the dented, charred steel cooking vessels processed only one kind of food.

Edgar's long black hair hung in dirty clumps; his mustache and beard were scraggly and unkempt; and his thick, gristly muscled arms were dotted with crude prison tattoos. As he worked, the only expression his hardened face could hold for more than a few seconds was a mean scowl. Preparation of the lamb was particularly annoying, as it was the only food that required brining before it was boiled. The extra step meant extra time he wasn't sleeping or drinking, which really pissed him off. He unzipped the brining bag, rinsed the lamb off in the sink, and tossed the discolored meat into a steel pot painted with a black number 21. The other meats were easy to prepare; he opened the refrigerator, unzipped each numbered bag, and dumped the contents into their corresponding numbered steel pot.

Pork, lamb, poultry, beef, and venison were precooked, or brined, the same day they were trucked in, with individual portions refrigerated and then reheated just before serving. It was critical to ensure that each meat was cooked through before being eaten. If an inmate died from bacterial poisoning, a lot of time, energy, and money would have been wasted. Getting a replacement product up to speed with camp routine was a big pain in the ass, and Edgar was far beyond the point of being able to tolerate new-inmate bullshit.

He unzipped the numbered vegetable bags and hacked up the contents of each with a rusty cleaver, making sure to wipe the cleaver clean with a cloth before moving to the next vegetable. Although it would only take seconds, he didn't rinse the onions, carrots, celery, peppers, and broccoli before scooping them up and dropping them into their corresponding numbered metal pots. He cooked the hell out of everything anyway, so there was no point.

Hilda always arrived at the kitchen fifteen minutes after Edgar. Since she met the supply convoys once a week, outside the fences, Edgar was tasked with cooking the meals. He was no fool—he would happily repeat the process four times every day, as long as he wasn't risking his neck outside the fence.

She rolled her steel food cart inside the kitchen, turned off the burners, and filled the cart with the five pots marked with white numbers. The stocky, ruthless female enforcer with deep scars in her right cheek and neck went about her job wordlessly and without looking at Edgar. Although they were technically friends and had screwed many times, there was no room for conversation or politeness when they were working.

Hilda tied her long, stringy blond hair back into a ponytail, retrieved a plastic bottle of water and a steel ladle from the sink, and then rolled her cart out of the kitchen, where she headed for the south gate and further, the female half of the yard.

Edgar strapped on a stained apron, verified that he had the proper bags of pharmaceuticals inside the front pocket, and loaded the five remaining numbered pots into his cart. He rolled the cart out onto the sidewalk of the administration area and inhaled deeply, cherishing the fresh air and relative freedom he now enjoyed. At one point, what seemed like a lifetime ago, he thought he would never get to see the sky or feel grass under his feet again.

As he crossed through the south fence gate and pushed the cart across the men's side of the yard, he thought about the first two feedings of the day and how smoothly they had gone. He could only hope this feeding was just as easy. In about six hours, he would be drunk and back in his room, a place where none of this would matter anymore.

* * *

4:35 P.M.

Jonah's tired eyes watched the sickly, pale heap of soggy broccoli get larger on his plate with each scoop from the rusty ladle. He was tired of smelling, seeing, and of course eating the putrid vegetable, but the penalty for refusing to eat was a violent beating that would render his body useless for at least a full day, and he liked exercise in the yard too much to risk it. The last time he refused a meal, he lost two teeth and had four ribs broken, but at least Dr. Selleck had given him extra orange pills for the pain.

He sat patiently at the feeding table, a plank of worn wood that was loosely secured to the cell wall with cheap rivets, and counted the scoops coming out of the steel pot, hoping today's ration was smaller than usual. A sliver of broccoli fell into Jonah's cup, splashing into the water, making the cloudy liquid even murkier. He would have to eat that piece too. Whatever came out of the pot must go in his body, or else.

The thin inmate's long hair was dirty blond and had a rough texture, just like his beard and mustache, both of which lacked any kind of routine cleaning and maintenance. Cheekbones poked out from his pale skin; his arms and legs were scrawny and weak. Many years of malnutrition had added artificial decades to his young life.

Edgar dug deeply into the steel pot and ladled more ugly sprouts of broccoli onto Jonah's crude metal plate. When the scoops exceeded six, Jonah gave up on trying to count them. He could barely read and only recognized a handful of words. Numbers, on the other hand, were an otherworldly concept that made his mind cramp. He watched the grotesque material pile up, silently wishing that somehow Barry's beef or Charlie's lamb had been accidentally mixed in with the broccoli.

Edgar's formidable size made Jonah's cell shrink. Each rectangular room in the men's barracks consisted of a narrow wooden platform that served as a bed; above the bed, in the corner of the ceiling, a haphazardly wired lightbulb that rarely worked; a hatch in the middle of the floor that, when opened, revealed a small hole through which bodily waste was disposed; the feeding table, a door with no handle; and lastly, every inmate's favorite feature, a window.

"That's plenty," Jonah whined to the colossal man looming over him, annoyed at the glut of broccoli that was being served.

Edgar raised an eyebrow, surprised at any glimmer of confidence, and dug deeply in the pot. He made sure that Jonah got an extra-special piece to offset the show of disrespect. A particularly gross sprout of broccoli came up with the ladle, making a nefarious smile bend across Edgar's face. He happily added it to the mushy green slop on Jonah's plate. "Enjoy," he said snidely, and banged the ladle against the pot, dislodging green and white remnants from the oversized utensil.

The hulking man with arms as thick as Jonah's waist picked up the filthy water bottle that served the barracks' entire ration of liquid for the day and turned to leave. Jonah gritted his teeth and cleared his throat, catching Edgar's attention. "My pills?" he asked, irritated. With every feeding, Jonah had pills, but he had to ask every time. Pills were the only reason he looked forward to feeding time.

Edgar searched his apron pocket and produced a handful of translucent bags filled with multicolored pills. He sorted through them and tossed the one marked with a "24" on the feeding table. The number matched the black digits painted onto the steel pot of broccoli, and also the number that had been sewn into the upper-left chest area of Jonah's gray burlap uniform. But unlike the steel pot and the number patch, the bag of pills wasn't stained with the blood of many cruel beatings.

Jonah hurriedly gathered the bag of colored pills. "Why do I have to ask every time?"

Edgar narrowed his eyes, making Jonah cringe. "If you want 'em, you'll keep asking." The large man walked into the hall and deposited the pot of broccoli onto the cart. He swung Jonah's cell door shut and locked it.

Jonah waited to hear the sound of the lock clicking into place before moving. He gently pushed himself up from the feeding table, tiptoed to the door, and peered into the hallway through a narrow, horizontally cut aperture. The prisoners referred to the opening as "the notch"; although universally used, no one could seem to remember where the term originated. Edgar and Headmaster Green used the notch to check in on the inmates from the hallway. The inmates used the notch to smell the other inmates' food. Jonah saw the nose tip of Richard, the inmate who occupied the cell directly across the hall from him, sticking out of his door notch.

Edgar opened the lock to the adjacent cell, turned to the food cart and collected a large steel pot painted with a black number 23, and then disappeared through the open door. Jonah turned his ear to the notch and listened carefully. When a clang from a steel pot rang out, he jammed his nose through the narrow opening and inhaled deeply. From the sound of it, Richard was doing the same thing.

A faint odor of boiled beef trickled in through the door notch. Reeling from the delicious smell, Jonah took in another lungful, fantasizing about the beef being served to Barry, the inmate who shared a wall with him. Jonah pressed his hand against the door, twisted his nose in the opening, and inhaled as deeply as possible.

Barry sat at his feeding table, dressed exactly like Jonah, but his uniform patch bore the number 23. He had long stringy hair, a wispy mustache, and an unkempt beard just like his neighbor. From a few paces away, the two young men looked identical, except Barry's hair was a shade darker.

Edgar hauled a cold, limp, discolored, and fatty chunk of beef out from the depths of the dirty pot and dropped it onto Barry's plate. The bony inmate stared down with familiar disgust. At least it wasn't a tail, he thought. Tails were the worst. "I'll have pills," Barry declared with a sniff of defiance.

Edgar breathed out, suppressing the urge to adjust Barry's attitude the old-fashioned way, and dug into his apron. After producing a bag of pills labeled with the number 23, he dropped it on the feeding table and filled the prisoner's cup with dirty water. Barry knew something was wrong with the pill count immediately.

"W-where's my other orange? I get two oranges."

"It's those or nothing, that's the choice," Edgar spat.

"Can you ask? I had two oranges, one blue, one red, and four brown."

Edgar grunted at the idiocy of such a suggestion. Ask? Eat shit, asshole. He shut Barry's door and locked it, unaware of the noses sticking out of the notches in the two cell doors behind him.

As Edgar rolled the cart farther down the hall to Charlie's door, Jonah withdrew his nose, knowing he could never get an adequate whiff of Charlie's lamb or Mitch's onions. He plodded over to his feeding table and sat down, giving in to the inevitable. He shoved broccoli into his mouth with his hands, going through the process in a semi-trance. It didn't have a taste anymore; it was just a substance he had to remove from the plate and consume. Soon, the pile of broccoli would be gone and he could turn his attention to his pills.

After the chunks were gone, he carefully tipped the plate back and slurped up the puddle of water and broccoli remnants, making sure to catch every bit of it. He dragged his hands down his hairy face, dredging broccoli bits from his beard, then popped what he had collected into his mouth. Edgar had thrown him in the hole more than once because too much broccoli was left on his mustache and beard. When his face and the plate were both cleaned, he completed the feeding ritual by licking the plate, first clockwise, then counterclockwise, until no sign of broccoli remained.

Feeling a weight lifted off his shoulders, Jonah took the plate to the door and slid it under, into the hallway. Edgar shouldn't have a problem when he checked it next feeding, unless the violence-prone man was in the mood to create one.

Jonah collected the bag of pills from the feeding table and brought it up to his eyes so he could double-verify something that looked very wrong. The bag held three orange, four blue, and one red. His face twisted with confusion, and he scratched his scalp with his free hand. Pinching the bag, he isolated one of the orange pills in the corner of the plastic, and looked at it skeptically. "Hmmm," he muttered to himself as thoughts slowly coalesced.

Jonah flopped on his wooden bed, making it creak and buckle, and opened the bag of pills. He separated the red pill from the others by shaking it carefully to the top of the bag. He dropped it into his palm and then tossed it into his mouth, immediately turning his attention to the remaining pills. The red pill made his heart beat faster, made his mind sharper, and also made him antsy. Jonah bounced his leg on the ball of his foot as the pill kicked in. Once again, he separated an orange pill from the others in the bag and looked at it with great interest.

"Extra orange," he mused quietly, his mind racing through the possible reasons. Sensations from the red pill flooded in; Jonah clenched his jaw and gritted his teeth as his thoughts sped up. Nothing at the Cydonia camp happened without a reason. Their routine had been dependable and unchanging for years, yet today he got an extra orange pill? He popped all four of the blue pills into his mouth at once. Blues didn't do anything as far as Jonah knew, but as with his food, if he was given pills, he had to eat them all.

A loud horn bleated twice, echoing down from the distant guard tower, making Jonah scramble to his feet and hurry to the window. A grid of rusty rebar impaired his view of the outside, but the layout of the yard was so familiar that he knew every inch of it by heart. Two horns meant it was time for women's exercise, his favorite time of day. He greedily ate two orange pills and licked his lips in anticipation of the forthcoming entertainment.

Four tired young women shambled out from behind the women's barracks and dispersed into the yard as two pairs. Just like the men, the women wore uniforms with patches numbered 20–24. As usual, the group was down one inmate. Jonah hadn't seen female 20 take exercise in months, ever since the last feast and her marriage to Mitch. Every day, Mitch asked Jonah if he had seen her in the yard, and every day Jonah disappointed him. None of them knew why she had vanished; the staff never explained anything to the inmates, so guesswork was their only option.

Hilda lurked in the background near the women's barracks, carefully watching the female inmates wander along the Lines of

Division. The rumor among the men was that Hilda had gotten the scars on her neck and face while fighting in a war, but Jonah never fully believed Charlie's stories, even if he had been in the camp years before Jonah, Richard, Barry, and Mitch had arrived.

Charlie was a pale, middle-aged ghost. His number 21 patch resembled his withered body and thinning gray hair. Like Jonah and Barry, he stared out into the yard through a web of steel bars and mindlessly ate from his bag of pills. Charlie was fixated on one female in particular, the same one that all three of them were staring at.

* * *

4:49 P.M.

Arva was by far the prettiest female in camp, a natural beauty with smooth golden skin; long, greasy brown hair; and bright green eyes. Ironically, she was the only person in camp who couldn't appreciate her beauty. Things like mirrors, makeup, and bathing were not words or concepts that inmates were exposed to.

She had been friends with Beth, a short, rail-thin girl with curly blond hair, since they rode into camp on a truck together years earlier. Beth had perfected the ability to make Arva and the others laugh, usually at the expense of Edith, the homely, long-faced girl with a slightly hunched back who wore number 24.

Edith's hair was bald in patches, and that, combined with her buck teeth and pudgy body, made her an easy target of ridicule. A long time ago, Edith would fire back at Beth with whatever insults she could manage, even if they didn't make sense, but defending herself just made Beth's attacks worse.

Although Beth always did the talking, Edith's hatred was mostly focused on Arva, who didn't deserve her beauty and the stares she got from the men. Edith could cope with Beth's mouth, but not Arva's looks—it was a daily reminder of how hideously ugly she was.

"I hear baldy through the wall all the time," Beth said, eyeing

Edith to make sure she was within hearing range. "It's like she's shitting herself while she sleeps, venison-farts right and left."

Beth mouthed several noises of digestive distress, gaining Edith's attention. Sue, the tall girl with dusky brown skin and curly black hair who was having a rare conversation with Edith, couldn't help but laugh.

The rotund, hunched-over girl turned away from Sue and plodded off toward the south fence, leaving the tall, dark-skinned inmate who wore the number 22 alone at the Lines. Edith couldn't help the noises she made at night; her body simply didn't agree with the venison she had to eat four times a day.

Arva laughed at the mocking too, but it was forced. She knew what was coming, and what she was about to risk. She turned and looked at male 24, who stared back at her through rebar. Something about him made her feel warm inside, even though their numbers didn't match and she would never be alone with him. A smile rose unintentionally; she couldn't look away from him.

Across the yard, inside the men's barracks, Jonah stood petrified. He couldn't believe it—female 21 was smiling at him, and he didn't know what to do. He smiled widely and awkwardly, and then began nodding enthusiastically while waving his hands, as if a bird struggling to gain flight. Somehow, he reasoned, nodding and waving would help.

Edith's jealous eyes tracked the exchange between Arva and male 24, and she didn't like it one bit. Edith had been staring at male 24 across the yard since their numbers had been assigned, but he never looked back. Maybe it was for the best. The one and only time the two inmates had locked eyes resulted in a look of disgust from male 24, and that look almost killed her. But Edith knew one day they would be married, his mind would change, and he would stare at her—and only her—until happily ever after. Headmaster Green had promised this to her many times; it would happen just like in the storybook he used to read to them. Edith wasn't going to let anyone, particularly Arva, take away what she had been promised.

Beth nudged Arva with an elbow, a silent reminder that they still had a plan to carry out. Arva tore her concentration from male 24, her face hardening as she deliberated over the task at hand. She carefully surveyed the yard, finding Edith plopped down on the grass by the south gate and Sue wandering along the east fence.

Hilda stood between the three groups of inmates, monitoring their activities while spinning a baton in her hand. She was carefully keeping track of Sue, who was walking parallel to the fence, eventually disappearing behind the women's barracks. Hilda slowly walked around the dilapidated wooden building, making sure that Sue remained an appropriate distance from the chain links, and briefly turning her back to Arva and Beth.

It was time. "Arva," Beth whispered, and motioned with her eyes.

"Come on," Arva said. She locked arms with Beth and walked toward the north fence, using the barracks to block Hilda's line of sight.

Edith leaned back on her hands, curiously watching her two enemies, taking internal notes on their every step just in case they broke the rules. Whenever either one of them misbehaved, Edith was always the first to tell Hilda. She smiled widely as memories flooded in, her lips tightening across buck teeth. Seeing Arva getting beaten was one of her most favorite things in the world.

As the two prisoners got close to the tall wall of chain links at the north end of the yard, Arva produced a folded piece of paper from her burlap pants and tossed it onto the men's side of the Lines of Division, less than a foot from the fence. The two young women veered away from the drooping barrier and quickly walked back along the Lines toward the barracks.

Edith couldn't believe what she had just seen. Throwing something on the men's side was just as bad as stepping across the Lines of Division, a taboo act associated with dire repercussions. Her devious smile suddenly vanished as she glanced at male 24; his eyes were still fixed on Arva.

Edith was tired of fighting off sadness and keeping hope alive. She longed for her marriage feast and the chance to be alone with male 24 in the marriage hut for seven days. Maybe she would tell Hilda about Arva throwing stuff on the male side of the Lines, and they could all watch her get her ass kicked, right here in the yard.

* * *

4:54 P.M.

Jonah wasn't looking at female 21 anymore. His gaze hadn't left the spot where the object landed. He was terrified at the idea of what it could be, feared the consequences of not telling, and frightened by the newness and suddenness of the event.

The horn on the guard tower screamed out, letting the camp know that the women's exercise was over, making Jonah jump. The extra orange pill shot out of the plastic pill bag he was holding and bounced across the floor of his cell toward the open excretion duct. Jonah dove after the pill and snatched it just before it could fall through the opening and into the sewage below. Relieved, he rolled to his back, rubbed the pill against his dirty uniform, and tossed it into his mouth. He got to his knees, closed the hatch to the excretion duct, fastened the flimsy sliding bolt, and stood up. Women's exercise was ending, so he might as well enjoy looking at the female inmates while he could.

Jonah reassumed his usual spot by the window to catch the last glimpses of female 21's body. The curves of her figure stirred something deep inside him, a rush of emotion that Jonah couldn't put into words.

Sue grudgingly led the line of inmates back into the women's barracks, with Beth and Arva following. Arva chewed nervously on her lip, stealing one final look at male 24 as she turned the corner of the building. She had endangered herself and her friends to benefit people she had never met, and was now left to wonder if the risk had been worth taking.

Ironically, she hadn't even written the note, and neither had Beth; they assumed that the author was a former inmate, as Beth had found it wedged between a loose floorboard and the wall of her cell. After they shared the contents of the message with Sue, she agreed to help them get the note to the men by distracting Hilda. After all that planning, and with the threat of severe punishment now hanging over all three of them, she hoped the men would be brave enough to follow the instructions in the note.

Edith, bringing up the rear of the line of inmates as usual, paused at the corner of the barracks and looked at male 24. He appeared to be looking back at her, and he wasn't revolted. On a whim, she decided to push her luck. She smiled and raised her hand, waving to him.

Jonah didn't move; the ugly girl obviously couldn't see the storm of anger that was bearing down on her from her flank, but he could.

Hilda's baton crashed down on Edith's raised hand, breaking at least one of her fingers. Crying out, Edith rolled to the ground as more pain was unleashed by the heavy baton. "What are you doing?" Hilda demanded as Edith sobbed and cradled her mangled hand. "The horn means go back inside!" she shouted and hit Edith across the ribs.

Hilda grabbed Edith by her thinning hair and dragged her to her feet. "Back to your cell, move!" Another blow from the baton drove Edith around the corner and out of sight.

Although the women had vacated the yard, Jonah knew they would soon be appearing in their windows. He leaned against the wall, his hand resting on a small metal vent above his bed. Wires from his cell lightbulb disappeared through the vent, snaking down into the unknown depths of the basement.

The extra orange pill was making him feel good—extra, extra good, in fact. He decided that he would look through the window until it was time to close the shutters.

A small insect crawled around Jonah's hand and disappeared through the metal vent. It steadily wriggled down the vertical shaft, following the spindly lightbulb wires, diving deeper into the stinking dark that lay below the barracks. The insect quickly scurried out from the vent the moment it reached the bottom of the small shaft, fleeing sudden gusts of malodorous breath and the nearness of large, misshapen fangs that glistened with gelatinized drool.

A large, monstrous shape huddled in the dark basement next to the vent, its spotty, pale snout pressed against the lightbulb wires. It breathed in deeply, savoring the smell emanating from the cell above it. Two burning red eyes blinked open and rolled as the odor filled its senses. It caressed the vent with sharp claws that extended from three long, scaly digits, craving the taste of flavored human. But it knew it had to wait—broccoli wasn't yet ready to be served; it needed to marinate more.

CHAPTER 2

The peaceful silence of early morning was shattered with three loud bleats from the guard tower horn, a piercing sound that awakened every living thing within two miles of camp.

Edgar opened the door to the men's barracks and stepped into the chilly hallway. Just like every morning, he checked Charlie's plate first. He stooped over, picked up the plate, and inspected it with meticulous care, making sure that no flecks of lamb were left from the previous day's fourth feeding. Once satisfied with the appearance of the plate, he put Charlie's empty pill bag into his apron pocket and unlocked the prisoner's door.

Charlie stood unmoving in the darkness, eyes wide open, shaking more than usual. Edgar knew it wasn't just the cold air that was making him shiver; something was amiss, but since he was smarter than all of the inmates combined, he would let things unravel naturally and dole out the beatings later. "Move," he grunted at the graying prisoner, who scuttled over to the shutters and opened the steel bolt. Charlie turned around, lowering his head as he shuffled out of his cell past Edgar and lined up next to the door that led out into the yard.

Edgar trudged to Barry's cell, where he repeated the process of scrutinizing the empty plate outside the door and ordering the inmate to open his shutters. Barry slid the bolt back from the shutters and gave them a push, then clicked his lightbulb off. The frail light was the only optional feature of the inmates' cells—they could have it on or off whenever they wanted. Problem was, when the light burned out, it could take months to replace, so use of the bulb was indulged sparingly.

By the time Jonah's shutters were opened and he had fallen in line behind Barry, Edgar could smell the stink of nervousness all over them. He turned to the cell across the hall and opened the door, where he went through the morning routine with Richard; the camp's youngest prisoner, who had been assigned the number 22, and celery as a food.

After Richard silently walked out of his cell and lined up behind Jonah, Charlie opened the door to the yard, and the inmates marched out. Edgar was last, baton in hand, waiting and watching for rules to be broken. Anxiety built in Jonah's chest with every step. He resisted the urge to run when his feet touched the grass of the yard. If he ran, Edgar would find whatever it was that female 21 had thrown onto the men's side of the Lines, and he would never get to see it.

The four men walked out into the yard, stopping inches from the Lines of Division. Jonah, Barry, and Charlie stared at the north fence, all wondering what the object in the grass could be. Arva, Beth, and Edith stood at their windows, staring out through rebar at the male inmates as Hilda secured their window shutters to the barracks wall.

Across the yard, Edgar was doing the same to the men's shutters while carefully keeping an eye on the male inmates. Something by the north fence was holding their attention.

Richard, confused, craned his neck to try to see what the others were staring at. "What are you guys looking at?" he asked in a loud hush.

"Should I go get it?" Jonah's eyes were locked on the small white object in the grass by the north fence.

"Get what?" Richard prodded.

Barry glanced at Edgar, who was tinkering with Jonah's window shutters; Edgar met Barry's eyes. He quickly looked away, huddling next to Richard, and lowered his voice to a cautious whisper, "Female 21 dropped something by the fence."

"So what?"

"She threw it on the men's side!" Charlie spat poisonously, but with instant regret. Edgar was staring right at him. "Uh, come on, guys, let's get exercise," Charlie said extra-loud. The inmates slowly crept along the Lines, drifting toward the north fence, conspicuously glancing at the mountain-sized enforcer, who was now leaning against the barracks.

The group of prisoners stopped twenty yards from the white object, which turned out to be a folded-up piece of paper. Richard scrambled behind Jonah to get as close as possible to the paper without leaving the group, "You guys watched her do it?" he squeaked.

"Yeah, it was pretty great," Jonah said, nervousness choking him.

"I'm so sick of my side of the barracks," Richard whined. "I see the fence and the forest and that's it. You guys get the yard! And women to look at!"

"You and Mitch get to see animals," Barry reminded.

"Through the shutters?" Richard asked sarcastically. "They only come out at night, stupid."

"Go complain to Edgar about your view; I'm sure he'd love to talk to you." Jonah smiled as Richard soured. The four thin men turned to find Edgar walking away from them, toward the south fence and the crudely dug ditches that the camp administrators used for isolation and punishment: the holes.

"He's getting Mitch," Charlie said, shaking his head. "Second time this month."

Edgar dragged the heavy stone off of the door-sized plank

and rolled it aside. He picked up one side of the warped wood, exposing Mitch, a tall, thin prisoner with pale white skin, closely cropped hair, cleanly shaved face and chin, and a uniform patch with the number 20. Mitch was squeezed crookedly into the deep, coffin-shaped ditch; Edgar hauled him to his feet with a violent tug and dragged him toward the men's barracks.

"He barely talks since he got married. I don't even see his nose in the notch anymore," Charlie said incredulously. They all knew that smelling the food of other inmates was almost as good as getting a taste.

Edgar marched Mitch across the yard and around the rear corner of the barracks. Mitch was bloody, bruised, dehydrated, and barely able to walk. He vacantly regarded the four scrubby prisoners standing near the Lines of Division as Edgar shoved him forward.

"He's got onions." Jonah shut his eyes and drooled over the idea. "I'd love to have onions; anything's better than broccoli."

"Refused his plate again, so Edgar kicked the shit out of him and threw him in the hole," Charlie said.

"We know—we all heard it, we all saw it," Barry said, irritated.

"I didn't see it," Richard complained. "I hate my side!"

With Mitch and Edgar out of sight, Jonah's attention fixed on the folded-up paper. He looked across the yard at female 21's cell window and found her looking at him. "Should I?" he asked the group, nodding toward the note.

"If they see you, you'll be in the hole for a week, at least!" Barry reminded him. As the dumbest of the five male inmates, Barry had spent considerable time in the hole, so he knew full well how much it sucked.

Hilda appeared from the far corner of the women's barracks and walked slowly toward the south fence gate, her back turned to the male inmates. Once she was through the gate and had vanished into the administration area, they resumed their disagreement.

Charlie angrily pointed at himself with this thumb. "Even if someone was to go pick it up, it would be me and not you, Jonah," he said spitefully, feeling his claim being infringed upon. "She's my number—we're getting married next."

"She stares at me a lot," Jonah challenged, making Charlie puff up defensively.

"She looks at me way more than you! And you've never even talked to her," he dismissed.

"None of us have!"

"But I will, soon," Charlie bragged smarmily. "Dr. Selleck said about two weeks from now."

As Jonah and Charlie stubbornly stared each other down, Richard tried talking them out of it: "What if the guards see you pick it up?"

Jonah was skeptical. "Are the guards even watching?" The prisoners turned their combined attention to the four guard towers, which showed no signs of life. Abandoned and rotting from the inside out, the towers seemed to be awaiting collapse.

"Guards" were a vaguely explained concept installed by Headmaster Green. The guards were terrifying, ruthless hunters that never got tired and somehow knew where the inmates were at all times. They were also invisible, apparently, as Jonah and the others had never actually seen them in person. The story was, if the prisoners escaped, the guards would kill them, or animals would. At least that's what the Headmaster said.

"I want to see what it is," Jonah announced suddenly and took off toward the folded paper. Charlie took two steps after Jonah, but cowardice shut down his motion. He was too afraid of misbehaving and giving them any reason to rescind his pending marriage to the most beautiful woman in the world.

"Hey, why's the fence so high, anyway?" Richard asked, distracted by the drooping, thirty-foot-high chain-link barrier. "It wasn't like that at the transition camp."

"I told you before: it keeps animals out," Charlie replied,

exhausted by Richard's inability to focus on anything for more than a few seconds.

Jonah snatched the folded-up paper off the ground and palmed it; then he sped back to the huddle of inmates, his heart racing from a spike of adrenaline. He felt like he had just eaten five red pills at once.

* * *

7:17 A.M.

Edith's broken fingers ached as she gripped the rebar grid that filled her window. She was mad at herself for not telling on Arva when she had the chance. The hunched-over, long-faced young woman looked to her right, through a small knothole in the wall she shared with Beth.

Beth was at her window, watching the male inmates just like every day. Edith decided to ruin her mood. "I saw what Arva did, and you," she said poisonously.

Instantly enraged, Beth stomped over to the wall and hit it with an open palm, making Edith back away. "You didn't see any- thing, liar!" She wanted to unleash her full fury on Edith but had to restrain herself. She walked back to her window and turned away from the knothole.

Edith smiled, knowing she had wormed her way under Beth's skin. "I saw Arva throw something on the men's side!" she shouted.

Beth's eyes zeroed in on the men's barracks, scanning for any sign of Edgar, the male enforcer, the only authority figure still within earshot. "No she didn't!" she said in a bitter, loud hush. "Now shut up!"

"I saw it, Beth," Edith said spitefully. "And I'm going to tell Headmaster Green you helped her." Beth tried to ignore the threat, but she wouldn't put anything past Edith. Her fate, and Arva's, depended on what the male inmates did with the note.

* * *

7:19 A.M.

Charlie crossed his arms, silently protesting Jonah's audacity, but he still wanted to see what the younger inmate was holding—they all did. The four shaggy, skinny men stood huddled in a circle.

Jonah checked to make sure that Hilda and Edgar were both still out of sight and then opened his palm, revealing a small folded-up piece of paper. He unfurled the paper, and the inmates gasped in unison. "Writing," he said nervously. He knew individual letters, but putting them all together was hard. Luckily, they had Richard, who could read entire sentences.

Barry shoved Richard next to Jonah. "Read it out loud," he said greedily.

Richard squinted at four words that were written in pencil: "Read spin-e of his-to-ry," he said, having to sound out the last word.

Jonah had an epiphany. "That's the brown book in the classroom, the big one."

"What's spin-e, though?" Barry wondered aloud, his dim mind struggling to think of viable options.

Charlie had a brilliant idea, one that would make him look smart and also put Jonah in his place. "I know what it means." He rubbed the dirty hair hanging from his chin, thinking through it. "She—you know, female 21, my number," he said into Jonah's face, "wants me to read this book, so we have things to talk about when we get married at the feast." He nervously tugged on his stringy beard, hoping the story made sense.

"You can't read," Jonah pointed out, obliterating Charlie's rationale.

"So Richard will read it for me," he defended arrogantly, and slapped Richard in the chest with the back of his hand, "right?"

Richard's eyes darted back and forth between the others, the idea of reading so much overwhelming him. His bouncing eyes finally settled on Charlie. "The whole book?"

One loud screech from the guard tower horn ended the conversation. Charlie stormed off toward the south fence, sulking and humiliated. Jonah's heart raced; they had to go, but he couldn't take the note with him.

Barry was thinking the same thing. "What are you going to do with it?" he gulped.

"Throw it over the fence!" Richard said excitedly, but after a synchronized look at the height of the fence, the three prisoners knew that was impossible.

"Eat it," Barry said with a grin. Jonah shrugged, thrilled with the suggestion. He jammed the paper in his mouth and started chewing.

"How does it taste?" Richard wiped drool from his mouth, wishing he had volunteered to eat it.

"Way better than broccoli," Jonah said through a full mouth. Besides being pasty and tasteless, the paper was a miraculous new experience.

"Give me some!" Richard whined, but Jonah was already gulping it down.

The sound of wood violently crashing against the exterior wall of the barracks instantly communicated something important to the inmates. Edgar had just kicked the barracks door open, and he was extra-angry. The force-feeding of Mitch must have taken a turn for the worse.

Jonah, Barry, and Richard started walking toward the south fence, where Charlie sat on the ground by the rusty gate. Edgar was stomping away from the men's barracks, dragging an even bloodier and bruised Mitch along with him. Onions dribbled out of Mitch's mouth as he stumbled alongside Edgar; yellow vomit streaked down his shirt.

Jonah now knew why Edgar was boiling with anger; Mitch had thrown up on him. After the one and only time Jonah threw up on Edgar, the baton almost took sight from Jonah's right eye.

"Hey! Get to the gate!" Edgar shouted at the inmates, making the three men pick up their pace.

As the group approached the south fence gate, Edgar pointed at Charlie with his baton. "Open it," he ordered. Charlie hopped to his feet and hurried to the gate, where he quickly unraveled the chain and swung the gate open.

Mitch struggled to maintain balance, but his knees buckled and his body crumpled. Edgar held Mitch up by one arm and then speared him in the gut with the end of his baton, knocking the wind out of him and forcing bile and blood to bubble from his mouth. The gangly inmate succumbed to unconsciousness when his shaved head hit the ground. Edgar grumbled as he picked up Mitch's legs and dragged him facedown across the grass. He found the four other inmates staring at him with wide eyes.

"Let's go!" Edgar snapped, jolting the prisoners into action. After dragging Mitch through the gate, he reached back and closed it, leaving the lock dangling from the chain. He rarely locked the south fence gate—same with Hilda on the female side. It wasn't like the inmates posed any kind of threat, and if the IILs wanted to get into the administration area, a small padlock wasn't going to stop them.

Jonah gleefully strolled through the administration area, following a winding sidewalk that took him and the other prisoners past small buildings made of thick concrete, sturdy chain-link fences, and interesting smells. He relished the smooth sensations that spread across the soles of his heavily callused feet every time he walked through this section of camp. Just like looking out of his window during women's exercise, trips to the administration building (and the classroom inside it) were something he looked forward to every day.

CHAPTER 3

The classroom floor was covered with something called a rug, a smooth, warm surface that Jonah got to step on whenever it was time for a lesson. Even if class ended with a beating, he still considered being in the classroom a treat. He scrunched his feet up on the rug and then relaxed them, smiling from the pleasurable feelings caressing his toes. Maybe one day, he thought wistfully, he could get a rug for his cell.

The five male inmates sat on plastic chairs in two rows in the middle of the rectangular room, facing an ancient blackboard that hung on the east wall. Narrow windows were interspersed throughout the chamber; each window was covered in rebar and cut into concrete as thick as a castle wall.

Edgar stood at the back of class holding a black rubber hose instead of his trademark baton. Rules of class were stricter than other camp rules, so more beatings were necessary. Frequent beatings meant delivering less damage per blow, so Edgar stuck to the hose, or his fist, while class was in session.

Each day, Headmaster Green, the merciless, imposing patriarch of camp, would stand behind his small desk, in front of the blackboard, and teach male and female inmates in alternating sessions. The males were dumber than the females and always caused more trouble, so the two sexes were never in class at the same time.

Headmaster Green's oily salt-and-pepper hair and mustache were trimmed and neatly combed, and his wide shoulders, thick chest, and short legs were clothed with an aging but clean recycled military uniform that had been tailored into a business suit. Wrinkled skin traversed his timeworn face; a hard life of war and stress had cut deep grooves into his brow and neck. His steely eyes had seen too many horrors, deaths, and tragedies to count.

"That's right, Charlie," the Headmaster smiled at the gray, pale prisoner, "Earth was created by magic. And Earth is a very nice place to live, isn't it? We're lucky to be here."

Charlie, pleased with himself, smiled and nodded. Jonah raised his hand.

"Jonah," Headmaster Green said skeptically as he read Jonah's body language. The thin little shit that stank like moldy broccoli was good at derailing the entire class from the topic at hand, and Headmaster Green wasn't in the mood today.

"How come we have to close the shutters at night?" Jonah asked carefully. The question wiped phony politeness from Headmaster Green's face. Jonah saw that his query wasn't being taken well. "You said something about stars during class last week? I think it would be nice if we could see stars… once." He shivered from the look that the Headmaster gave him.

"We've had this kind of question asked recently, haven't we?" the grizzled authority figure asked the class scornfully.

"But yesterday, Barry asked why he has to eat beef every day, and why I have to eat broccoli, and Richard has to eat celery, and why—"

"We all remember, Jonah," Mitch's eyes cracked open as Headmaster Green sharply cut Jonah off. "We all know the other men's food. We know why we have to eat what we eat, and why we have to close the shutters at night."

Barry and Jonah exchanged confused looks. Charlie pretended that he was thinking about the answer.

Richard thought he had an answer but didn't. "We do?"

"We serve the greater good!" the Headmaster said happily. "Now Jonah, one more unpleasant question like that and Edgar will beat you with the hose," he warned blandly.

Jonah turned and considered Edgar, weighing the choices in his mind, and then turned back to the Headmaster. "How many times?"

Headmaster Green clapped his hands, breaking their concentration. "OK, question and answer time is over, so let's get into a new topic, something I think you'll all find interesting." The Headmaster picked up a nub of chalk and wrote "*history*" in sloppy cursive across the cracked, flaky blackboard. "History—it means things that happened in the past."

He put the chalk down and chose a book from a small row that ran congruently under the chalkboard, a large brown leather tome with the word "History" printed vertically down its spine. Headmaster Green didn't notice the extreme attention that the four inmates were paying to the book; he cracked it open and leaned against the desk as Jonah, Barry, Charlie, and Richard stared at the pages with wide eyes. Mitch, unconscious and drooling, was splayed out in his chair, his body inches away from sliding to the floor.

"Let's say… over a thousand years ago, some people called the Romans owned the Earth. They bought it from the Greeks, who owned it a long time before that. Then—"

Jonah raised his hand, simultaneously sidetracking the lesson and angering Headmaster Green. "Jonah?" the Headmaster asked through clenched teeth.

Jonah looked over his shoulder at Edgar, who glared back at him. "Who owns the Earth now?"

Headmaster Green melted back into his "pleasant" façade. "A

very smart group of people own it; business men and women that fund all twelve of the Cydonia camps. Their money pays for your food, your pills, the staff, and our facility here at Cydonia 6." He grandly waved his free hand at the surrounding environment.

The inmates were adults physically, but Headmaster Green knew that he had to explain things to them as if they were infants. Once in a while, just to fuck with them, he would throw in words way over their heads. "These men and women are known as the Global Conglomerate," he said with a smirk.

The four conscious inmates puzzled over the explanation. Jonah slowly raised his hand again. Headmaster Green strangled Jonah with his eyes. "Question and answer time is over," he said sternly, his hairy lip twitching. Jonah took his hand down, disappointed.

"Thank you." He gathered the nub of chalk again and wrote "Columbus" across the blackboard in block letters. "Thousands of years ago, a man named Columbus flew an airplane called Apollo, high into the sky," he said, using his hand to model what he was talking about, "all the way to the moon."

Barry's hand shot up, which was followed by anxious noises that indicated he badly wanted to be acknowledged. Headmaster Green breathed out and put the chalk back in the tray. He dusted his hands off as he slowly walked back to the desk and leaned against it. "Barry," he said calmly.

Barry didn't take his hand down. "Has anyone ever flown an airplane from Earth to a planet, like Mars?"

Taken aback by Barry's unexpected and only slightly flawed mental acuity, the Headmaster glanced at Edgar, silently communicating the need to get ready. Edgar walked within two paces of the rows of seated inmates. For some reason, the prisoners had remembered the lesson he had given on the solar system with unnerving accuracy, even Barry the imbecile. He decided then and there that stars and planets would be permanently removed from the lesson plan. "Sure, why not," he dismissed.

Barry's hand still anxiously waved, "Uh, Headmaster Green? I wanted to also ask about my extra orange pill. I like orange pills, so could I have two again instead of one?"

The war-hardened Headmaster nodded to Edgar, who bulled his way through the chairs and hit Barry across the back of the skull with the hose. Mitch was thrown to the ground in the wave of activity, the impact rudely rousing him from his stupor.

Barry fell to the ground and rolled into a ball as more blows from the hose crashed down on him. After a sufficient amount of wallops were doled out, Edgar jerked Barry to his feet and hauled him out of the classroom, letting the door slam behind them. Mitch tipped Barry's seat back to upright and sat down on it, directly in front of the Headmaster.

When things quieted down, Headmaster Green smiled as he addressed the class. "Now, let's continue." To his disbelief, Mitch quickly raised his hand. "Yes… Mitch?" the Headmaster cautioned darkly.

"Where are the guards?" Mitch's question hung in the air, drawing worried looks from Jonah, Charlie, and Richard. The guards were a taboo subject; everyone knew that.

Headmaster Green pursed his lips as he considered the bloody, bruised, thin little mess staring back at him. The open display of rebellion would have to be dealt with, he thought grimly. He put the history book under his arm and leaned away from the desk. "I think we've had enough of a lesson today. Let's spend the remaining time in free study." He strolled out of the classroom gritting his teeth. He hated them a little more every time he gave a lesson.

Jonah was confused over the Headmaster's behavior, but once he was gone, being quiet didn't matter anymore. "Mitch! What's wrong with you? How could you ask that?" he snapped, knowing that all five of them could get beaten because of Mitch's insolent behavior.

Mitch turned his bleeding face toward Jonah, his eyes drooping with opiate-induced numbness. "I've never seen the guards, have you?"

CHAPTER 4

Jonah squeezed his head with both hands, covering his ears to drown out the sounds of impact and agony coming from next door, but the loud crashes and soulful wailing were too intense to ignore. He was as far as possible from the activity, on his bed, facing the wall, cowering in wait for his turn, but he could feel the vibrations of violence as if he were in the room with them. Sometimes Edgar hurt only the inmate that broke the rules, other times he hurt them all; today was a toss-up.

Barry had been taken from class, thrown in the hole for a handful of hours, and then dragged back into his cell for feeding. The time between those events unfolded as usual: Edgar served the inmates their food, and then they closed the shutters. An hour before darkness fell, Barry's punishment began. Jonah hoped the malicious enforcer would be too tired from the session to take on someone new.

A heavy thud shook the wall, then silence followed; the combination of sounds meant that Barry had been beaten into unconsciousness. Jonah took his hands away from his ears and sat up, listening for clues as to who would be Edgar's next victim, if one were to come. He heard Barry's cell door being locked and then footsteps in the hallway.

Mitch, Edgar's favorite human punching bag, was typically next, regardless of who had gone first. Mitch had been causing a lot of problems since his marriage to female number 20, setting off a self-destructive streak that now seemed like it would never end. As his misbehavior increased, so did the violent pastings and isolation time in the hole.

Mitch hadn't been able to cope with the reality of his diet returning to onions after a seven-day hiatus, but it was the disappearance of his opposite number that really started his pattern of disobedience. No one had seen female 20 for months, ever since the feast. The short woman with black hair, beige-colored skin, and a wide, moon-shaped face didn't exercise anymore, and she never went to class with the others. Sharing a bed and a feeding table with her for seven nights had changed Mitch considerably, his sudden infatuation taking the rest of the male inmates by surprise. Before the feast, Mitch was a talkative, bubbly person. Afterward, he was a melancholy, miserable mess. Every conversation eventually led to the female and their days together. The memory he talked about most frequently was eating pork, female 20's assigned food.

Although Jonah longed for the change to routine, he dreaded the idea of being locked up in the marriage hut with his opposite number for an entire week. The idea of seeing her close up, and having to share a bed with her, made him gag.

Jonah got up from his bed and crept past his feeding table, where a plate of cold, discolored broccoli waited for him. He tiptoed to his door and peered through the notch; Edgar was in the hallway, cleaning blood from his fists with a towel.

Edgar unsnapped a ring of keys from his belt, sorted through the keys, and walked down the hallway, out of Jonah's sight. Jonah shifted his angle and looked directly across the hall, where he found Richard's eyes dancing in the door notch. Richard was too short to see through the narrow window without having to balance on his toes. Since neither man could see the cells at the end of the hall, they had to just listen.

Keys jingled, a cell door swung open, and then Edgar cried out in sudden pain. Jonah pushed his face as hard as possible against the notch, his eyes desperately searching for clues into what was happening. Grappling, heaving breathing, and grunts thudded though the hallway; finally, Jonah could see them, rolling on the ground near the food cart. Mitch punched Edgar in the cheek and followed with an elbow to his nose. The vision of an inmate pummeling Edgar was surreal; for a moment, Jonah wondered if he was dreaming.

Mitch's rebellion was an epic event, but very short-lived. Edgar shifted under the skinny prisoner, freeing his right arm. His massive fist shot straight up, crashing against the underside of Mitch's chin. The powerful blow knocked the gangly inmate off of him as if he were a bug being swatted. Edgar stood up, breathing heavily, and reached to retrieve his baton from the ground.

Mitch, who had been feigning unconsciousness, hiked up the right leg of Edgar's pants and bit the meaty portion of his calf as hard as his discolored teeth and damaged jaw could manage.

"Ahhhh!!! You fucker!" Edgar shouted, and swung his baton down, hammering the crown of Mitch's head with a loud crack. One of the prisoner's teeth was left embedded in his leg muscle. Thick blood oozed from Edgar's leg as he plucked the tooth out of his calf; he hobbled next to Mitch, who was also losing blood, and retrieved a syringe from his apron. Whimpering, the large man knelt next to Mitch and administered the injection.

The good thing about Edgar's syringe was that it numbed pain instantly; the bad part was that the needle turned your mind into jelly for a number of hours. The injection usually preceded the inmate being dragged out into the yard and thrown into the hole for isolation; but the shutters were closed, and everyone knew that Edgar only threw inmates in the hole before dark. Fresh blood in the yard at night would attract animals, and animals could kill them all if they got inside the fence.

Edgar picked up Mitch's drooping body and threw him over his shoulder. Jonah's eyes widened when he saw Edgar limp toward the barracks door; the sound of the door shutting behind him meant that the impossible had just occurred.

"What's happening?" Richard hissed in a loud whisper.

"He took Mitch out!" Jonah replied incredulously.

"Out?" the younger prisoner's eyebrows furrowed.

"Outside!"

"No!" Like Jonah, Richard couldn't comprehend it.

"Yes!" he shrieked back, annoyed. "I just saw!"

"It's night, though," Richard mumbled. "Are you sure?"

Frustrated with the conversation, Jonah ran to his shuttered window and aligned his left eye with a small crack between the panels, but he saw nothing but dim light. For a split second, he considered opening the shutters, but that would break one of the most unbreakable rules of camp.

Jonah leaned against the rebar web covering the window, fingers wrapping around the steel, thoughts turning on him yet again. *How did I end up here? Why here, and why me?*

"Can you see them?" Richard's voice echoed from the hallway.

Jonah hung his head and wept into his hands.

CHAPTER 5

Chilly dew on the grass made Jonah's feet numb, but at least on cold days he could go for exercise wrapped in his burlap blanket. Charlie was wrapped up in an identical fashion; both men stood at the Lines of Division, silently breathing out clouds of steam. Even though it was summer, the air was still frigidly cold.

After Edgar had opened their doors and lined up the inmates, he split Richard and Barry off from Jonah and Charlie, and escorted the two inmates to the administration area. Barry walked in a stooped-over hunch, with a limp. Edgar's limp had been less noticeable, but his calf injury had made the huge man extra-surly all the same; Jonah and Charlie both felt lucky to have avoided protracted interaction with him this morning.

"Why did Richard go to the administration area?" Charlie suddenly asked.

"Doctor's appointment," Jonah murmured.

Charlie nodded. "How about Barry?"

"Treatment probably," he shrugged.

A large, pale blur barreled through the shrubs near the north fence, making both inmates' heads swivel to follow it. They exchanged confused looks and then slowly walked along the Lines toward the commotion. The prisoners stopped two feet from the tall chain-link fence and scanned the forest beyond it, searching for any sign of animals.

Something suddenly moved behind a wall of shrubs, breaking branches and crushing overgrowth along the way. It was staying in the shadows, but they could still see it. A leathery, white-skinned creature twice the height of Edgar, and three times as wide, was in the forest—only twenty yards from the fence.

A grotesquely misshapen, pale, humanlike face abruptly pushed through the bushes and locked eyes with the inmates. Its wide head moved back and forth as it studied the two men; a pair of tusks jutted out from its mottled mouth, and large scars of melted skin traveled the length of its neck. It didn't like the sunlight and retreated into the shadows each time a gust of wind shifted the canopy of trees above it. Without provocation, the animal quickly ducked back into the forest and disappeared into the maze of trees.

Jonah and Charlie smiled widely at each other, excited over seeing something new. Animals never came out during the day; this was the first time either of them had seen one. Unlike the guards, now they knew animals were real.

* * *

7:16 A.M.

Barry leaned painfully against the wall, each movement pushing daggers of agony through his ribs. Dr. Selleck had stitched a gash above his eyebrow, wrapped his torso in tape, and given him six orange pills for pain. In some ways, the beating he had endured the previous night was worth extra pills—until they were gone. He had eaten the first pill before leaving the doctor's office, and another upon sitting down. Barry mulled over the idea of having a third but decided against it. Three orange in a row might knock him out.

Richard was with the doctor now, so Barry had to wait on the uncomfortable wooden bench in the hallway until the younger inmate's appointment was done. Edgar didn't like making two trips, and Barry needed to get back on the enforcer's good side so that his ribs could heal.

He could hear voices in the Headmaster's office but couldn't make out what they were saying. Even if he could, Headmaster Green frequently used big words that went way over Barry's lice-infested head. The voice that was currently speaking on the other side of the door was unknown to him. The tone was stern and clear, just like the voice of Headmaster Green, but deeper and more casual sounding.

* * *

7:17 A.M.

"Do you remember Cydonia 11?" the Governor asked, absently swirling the ice cubes in his scotch.

Headmaster Green raised an eyebrow. "*Remember* it?"

"You did time with Headmaster Krupps, if I remember correctly."

The Headmaster nodded slowly. He didn't like where this was going. Any visit from the Governor was cause for alarm, but he had a feeling it was about to get much worse than he had first thought.

"They were all slaughtered—Krupps, inmates—by a Pale Giant. An inmate was out at night, very late apparently, and tried to touch the Giant through the fence. So of course it ripped the fence down, the towers too, and then destroyed everyone and everything. I wish I had pictures to show you; it literally looks like the camp was bull-dozed flat.

"And now the Masters want a new lot, *at no cost*," the Governor emphasized. "They cited the indemnification clause in the contract, specifically our negligence in not maintaining the products correctly. The Masters have lawyers now, if you can believe it. They cannot be held accountable for the actions of the Giants, and since their precious flavored humans were taken away from them, we have to make them whole.

"You have the report—get the details from that—but," the Governor leaned forward, his cologne overpowering the Headmaster, "we have to start dealing with the loss immediately." He tipped back the glass of scotch, finishing it, and placed it on top of the manila folder he had left on the Headmaster's desk.

Headmaster Green smiled. Here it comes, he thought to himself.

"With Cydonia 11 off the map, we're one camp short on payment. The territories won't accept being shorted, so we have to divide the responsibility of the missing share among the remaining eleven camps," the Governor said casually.

Headmaster Green contained his disbelief and anger by pouring himself another glass of vodka. He had to keep his hands busy, or else he might throttle the Governor and toss his corpse into the basement so the Masters could have a snack. "Want another one?" He grabbed a fresh bottle of scotch from the cabinet and held it up expectedly.

"No, it's long ride back."

Headmaster Green flashed his rehearsed smile. "So… dividing up responsibilities; I assume equally, even though Cydonia 1 and 2 are double our capacity."

The Governor sighed, irritated at having to bargain with scum like this in person. "We'll do it by total inmate count, as of the day of the massacre, agreed?"

Headmaster Green nodded, respectfully conceding to the new arrangement. "Absolutely; you're the Governor, I'm just a Headmaster."

The Governor stood and retrieved his blazer from the back of the chair, slowly slipping it on so as not to create wrinkles. "One more thing, Green: I don't want to hear about abuse of the bonus. It's been happening in other camps, but I don't want it here. We're too close to the border, and if word gets back home…" he trailed off, his eyes communicating disaster.

Headmaster Green stepped into the doorway and turned the door handle. "Of course, only one per couple; when I get the payment, I'll com-link your office and arrange for pickup…" His words fizzled out as the door opened; Barry was sitting on the bench across from the entrance to his office, wrapped in bandages.

The Governor stepped out into the hall and stopped, staring at the shaggy inmate. Barry stood up, his bruised, swollen, and bloody mouth gaping open in wonder. Almost toe to toe, the Governor and Barry examined each other, the Governor disgusted, Barry fascinated.

Barry couldn't get over the cleanliness of the man standing before him. There weren't any patches of material on his jacket or pants, and his shoes were shiny and spotless. "Who are you?" he blurted, confused.

"No one," the Governor replied scornfully, and looked back at the Headmaster. "Green?" he prodded.

Headmaster Green pushed Barry back down onto the hallway bench. "Right this way, Governor." As the Governor began walking, the Headmaster turned back to the stupefied inmate. "Get to class!" he snapped.

"I'm waiting for Richard—he… he's getting a haircut, I think," Barry stammered.

Headmaster Green dismissed the conversation as if shooing away an annoying fly, and opened the main door to the administration building for the Governor. The door thudded behind the two men, leaving Barry looking curiously after them.

* * *

7:25 A.M.

Jonah and Charlie wandered along the Lines of Division, slowly closing on the hole, where Mitch still lay trapped under a warped plank of wood. Beyond the main gate, out along the gravel road, they saw Hilda pushing a deep plastic tub that rolled on one broad, rubber wheel. They broke off at an angle, walking adjacent to the men's barracks and directly toward the western fence. They stopped two feet from the chain links and wordlessly watched the female enforcer as she approached the main gate.

Hilda carefully set the rolling tub down near the gate and produced a ring of keys. After unlocking the gate, she swung it open and pushed the tub through, then locked the gate behind her. She disappeared behind the buildings in the administration area, but the distinct sound of the tub rolling over sidewalk could still be heard.

Jonah and Charlie walked over to the south fence gate and waited. It happened once a week, and it was the only time Hilda ever looked at the male inmates. Hilda turned a corner between buildings and came into sight, the large plastic tub's wheel clicking over the concrete as she pushed it. She glanced at the two skeletons standing behind the men's south fence gate, but passed them without another thought. Jonah and Charlie stared at the contents of the tub as it rolled by; it was bulging with plastic bags full of the camp's assigned foods.

"Wonder where she gets it from," Charlie mused.

"The Headmaster said magic, but he always says that," Jonah said, annoyed.

"Maybe the forest?"

"I think trucks bring it."

Jonah's explanation befuddled Charlie. "Trucks?"

"Like the things that brought us here from the transition camp—big metal machines with wheels? Don't you remember?" Jonah spat, irritated.

"I can't remember that far back anymore," he replied softly.

"They had a bunch of food in it when they dropped us off." Jonah's thoughts were distant. "First time I ever saw real food," he ruminated.

Headmaster Green and the Governor suddenly appeared to their left, walking along the sidewalk toward the main gate. Jonah and Charlie watched, stunned, as the two men strolled past. "Good morning," the Headmaster said.

"Hi, Headmaster. Who's that?" Charlie pointed to the Governor.

"Get back from the gate!" the Headmaster barked, making Jonah and Charlie retreat a step.

* * *

7:28 A.M.

Headmaster Green wrung his hands and sneaked a look to his flank, making sure that the inmates were out of earshot. The main gate was looming, so he had to spit it out. "Did you, uh, see anything on your way in?" he asked nervously.

"What should I have seen?" the Governor carefully replied.

"Something that shouldn't be happening," the Headmaster shivered. "The Giants are getting active in the daylight. I've seen them a few times."

"It's their territory; they do what they want," the Governor shrugged.

Headmaster Green pulled his keys from his pocket and slowly tinkered with the lock. "But I can't—I won't—lock myself up day and night. I came here to get away from that."

The Governor breathed out, frustrated, knowing that the former felon was taking his time with the lock on purpose. "The contract says shutters closed at night. If they attack in the day, it's war again. Neither side wants that.

"Look, if you think something's about to happen, get on the com-link. Border security is close enough for an evacuation," he said as he patted Headmaster Green on the shoulder. The words were meant to be reassuring, but they both knew the truth. If something happened, there wouldn't be time to call anyone.

The Headmaster slipped the lock off the hasp of the main gate, opened the gate, and then stood back, letting the perfumed man with polished shoes amble through. The Governor could walk anywhere and do anything he pleased inside IIL territory—he was on the list of untouchables, so it was easy for him not to be afraid.

Headmaster Green shut the gate and locked it as the Governor disappeared into the forest, hoping in the back of his mind that the Giants would ignore the rules for once and kill the arrogant asshole while they had the chance.

* * *

7:29 A.M.

Jonah and Charlie balanced on their toes next to the western fence, straining to see the man in clean clothes that had been talking to the Headmaster, but he had walked into the forest too quickly for them to get a good look. Behind them, Edgar opened the creaky south gate and left it ajar, which meant his trip into the yard would be a quick one. Jonah and Charlie turned from the fence as Edgar trudged angrily toward the hole.

Long, sweaty black hair hung in Edgar's face as he rolled the large stone back and then lifted the warped plank, throwing it aside. He yanked Mitch out of the hole by his frail arm and left him standing on two wobbly legs.

Jonah and Charlie let Edgar vanish beyond the south fence gate before speed-walking over to Mitch, who was barely maintaining balance. His bloody, black-and-blue face was still numb from a large dose of sedatives, but he was awake enough to give them answers.

"Why did you do that last night?" Charlie demanded.

"Felt like it." Bloody drool dribbled down Mitch's chin as he staggered toward the men's barracks.

"You're going the wrong way—we still got class," Jonah admonished.

"Oh," Mitch spun around, nearly falling over, and staggered in the opposite direction.

"So hey," Charlie licked his lips with anticipation, "what was it like being outside at night like that?"

"Did you see stars?" Jonah interjected excitedly.

"I saw…" The tall, gangly, beardless inmate with a close-ly-shaved head stopped walking, and swayed back and forth as he cracked open foggy memories. "I saw two moons."

Jonah and Charlie exchanged confused glances. "There's only one moon, Mitch. The Moon, the one Columbus flew his plane to," Jonah said condescendingly.

"Hmm, maybe you're right," Mitch agreed lazily.

Charlie grabbed Mitch's shoulder, shaking him to gain his attention. "You missed it! We saw this guy, who was dressed really crazy, and he was talking to Headmaster Green, and his clothes were clean-clean, like really clean."

"And he was taller than Headmaster Green," Jonah added.

Charlie shot an angry look at Jonah. "I was getting to that, Jonah," he spat.

The guard tower horn bleated once, announcing that it was time for class. Jonah and Charlie buttressed Mitch as they walked toward the south fence gate and continued to rattle off observations about the strange man in clean clothes that had been talking with the Headmaster.

CHAPTER 6

Headmaster Green silently steamed, anger expanding into fury. He gritted his teeth as he looked from inmate to inmate, starting with Jonah, who smiled back at him, totally ignorant of the storm gathering behind the Headmaster's snarl.

Next was Barry, the spineless moron. Barry resembled a freshly wrapped mummy, with bandages wrapped in several layers around his skull, covering his cheek, lips, and jaw. Headmaster Green pushed back the desire to add to Barry's collection of wounds and turned his eyes to Mitch, a lifeless scarecrow that was being held upright in his chair by the Headmaster's favorite henchman, a former assassin for the Mafia and a convicted mass-murderer.

Edgar let go of a knot of Mitch's burlap uniform, and the thin prisoner slid down in his chair, his shaved head bobbing lifelessly as he slowly collapsed. Before he could slide onto the rug, Edgar hauled him back upright by his collar, and the process repeated.

In the front row sat Richard, whose appearance was so confusing that it evoked a muted sound of disbelief from the Headmaster. Richard's entire head was shaven neatly in half, including his adolescent beard and mustache, with baldness encompassing the right hemisphere of the youngest prisoner's cranium and face. Even Richard's right eyebrow was missing. The most irritating thing was that he had no idea that he looked unusual.

"What happened?" Headmaster Green demanded, staring daggers at Richard.

Richard looked over his shoulder, searching for the person that the Headmaster was addressing, but found the back of the classroom empty. He nervously pointed to Mitch and hopefully raised his remaining eyebrow.

"No, Richard, I'm talking to you," the Headmaster said poisonously.

"What happened?" Richard recited, unsure of the meaning behind the question.

"Your head, your face!" Oblivious, Richard touched his face, then his head, not understanding. "One side is bald—even your eyebrow's gone!" the Headmaster seethed.

"My hair?" Richard could hear the Headmaster's teeth grinding, so he knew he was on the right track. "Dr. Selleck did it. I asked him to cut it like Mitch; I had too many bugs."

A thick stream of drool dribbled out of Mitch's mouth; Headmaster Green massaged his forehead, suppressing the urge to kick Mitch in his unconscious face. "Only married couples get their heads shaved; Mitch is married. You know this, Richard."

Richard paused, the gears of his mind grinding at top speed. "I guess that's why he only did half?" The explanation made perfect sense to him, but he could tell that his responses, in general, weren't sitting well with the Headmaster.

Headmaster Green closed his eyes, calming himself. His eyes popped open after a few seconds and quickly swiveled to Edgar. "Can you tell the doctor I'd like a word with him, please?"

Edgar slowly nodded and exited the classroom; the eyes of all four conscious inmates curiously followed him. Now lacking support, Mitch slid off his plastic chair and onto the floor; everyone ignored him.

Headmaster Green retrieved the large, leather-bound history book from the stack under the chalkboard and set it on his desk. "I apologize for not being able to continue our lesson on history today, gentlemen, but I have some urgent business to attend to now." He stood up and straightened his jacket, knowing that the next few minutes would be frustratingly long.

"Practice reading a few sentences on the first page, and tomorrow you'll read out loud to the whole class." Headmaster Green checked his watch and flashed his finest fake smile. "That's fifty-one minutes of free study time." He stepped over Mitch's unmoving body and exited the classroom, slamming the door behind him.

When the sounds of walking disappeared beyond the door, Jonah, Barry, Charlie, and Richard swarmed the Headmaster's desk. Jonah picked up the history book and flipped randomly through pages with the other three looking over his shoulders. He arbitrarily stopped at two pages in the middle of the book and placed it flat on the desk so that they could all look at the individual words. Charlie didn't like his viewing angle, so he usurped Richard's position by elbowing him to the rear of the group.

Bloody saliva seeped out from Barry's bandaged mouth and dribbled over the plastic sleeves that covered the book's pages. "Sorry," he said, embarrassed, and wiped his swollen lips.

Jonah smeared Barry's blood off the pages with his cuff and traced the words on the page with his finger, his brow furrowed in concentration. "I don't see 'spin-e' anywhere. The note said 'spin-e of history,' right?" he asked the men huddled behind him. Getting no response except for a noncommittal nod from Richard, he picked up the book and turned it in his hands, examining every inch of it. He put it down and looked at it lengthwise.

Barry fiddled with the top end of the spine of the book, where the glue had come away, using his long, dirty fingernail as a probing device. "Hey, this is loose right here—see it, guys?"

Jonah slapped Barry's hand away and picked up the book, opening it in the middle again, but this time he placed it face down on the Headmaster's desk. The leather-like material covering the spine of the book pulled away, creating an opening between the book binding and the cover. The heads of the four inmates collided as they simultaneously tried to see what was inside the newly created cavity.

Jonah stuck his pinky nail into the opening and scraped it against the binding. Eventually, he felt his nail snag on something. He carefully dragged the prize out from the book binding, his heart beating loudly in his chest. A discolored square of folded paper emerged from the book spine and fell onto the Headmaster's desk. The stunned inmates stared at it for a moment, exhilarated by its presence. Jonah warily picked up the paper and unfolded it.

"More writing," he announced solemnly. The words were strangely written, and Jonah knew right away that he didn't know some of them. "Here," he handed the paper to Richard, the group's best reader.

Richard felt flop sweat accumulate on his half-bald head, lip, and chin as he scanned the individual letters. After shoving some letters together in his mind, he felt confident enough to read it to the others, in one long, run-on, robotically phrased sentence: "Do not eat drink at feast mon-sters live below us me name Ed me number one six me food brock-li." Richard wrinkled his oddly trimmed face up, not understanding what he had just read. He reread it quietly to himself as the others chewed over the words.

"His food is broccoli," Jonah realized with a gulp.

"*Was* broccoli, and that could be like… sixteen, not one-six." Although Charlie was far from intelligent, he could count. "Fifteen through nineteen left a long time ago, except me." Charlie shivered from the memory. "Bumped me up twice," he said bitterly. "Ed left, without even being married," he spat. "Then they bumped me up from eleven to nineteen, then nineteen to twenty-one!"

"Did he have my cell?" Jonah croaked, afraid of the answer. The idea of another man having his cell, and his food, spooked him.

Charlie nodded. "Maybe you'll leave early, too."

The thought simultaneously warmed Jonah's stomach and made him queasy. Getting out? Ironically, he had never really thought about it; if he were released soon, he wouldn't be prepared.

Richard rubbed the bald half of his skull, not liking the thoughts that were bubbling up. He slammed the note down on the Headmaster's desk; all eyes turned on him. "This says we shouldn't eat food at the feast!" he exclaimed, offended.

Jonah rejected the idea instantly. "But we can have whatever we want!" he said incredulously.

"It says right here, do not eat drink at feast." Richard pointed to the words on the scribbled note.

"What about this word, 'mon-sters'?" Barry's dirty index finger pointed to the letters as he sounded it out.

Richard shrugged. "I don't know, could be a..." His sentence was left hanging; no ideas sprang to mind.

"I think it's something about an inmate," Barry explained, trying his best to sound smart and failing miserably. "Headmaster called me a monster once, when I shit my pants during a lesson."

A shadow silently opened the classroom door and crept in behind the group as they talked. The prisoners were huddled around the history book, but it was upside down on the desk. The dark shape waited, observing them, seeing what would transpire while it was unnoticed; a bigger shadow came in behind the first, looming in the doorway.

"What are you doing!?" Headmaster Green suddenly boomed, making the inmates jump and shudder. They spun nervously toward him, terrified. He had caught them in the middle of something, and from their reaction, they had been misbehaving.

Jonah hid his hands behind his back, knowing that if the note were discovered, the beating he got would be long and painful. Headmaster Green might even take away his pills. Richard stood to Jonah's left, with Charlie on his right. Jonah searched the table with his right hand, blindly groping for the note as his eyes remained fixed on the two authority figures about to kick his ass.

"N-nothing," Charlie babbled, overcome by the need to defend himself.

Jonah's fingertips grazed paper; he picked up the note and crumpled it into a ball.

Headmaster Green steamrolled toward Charlie and punched him in the stomach, the blow eliciting a familiar and unique gasp of pain that they had all heard many times. Charlie dropped to his knees, fell to his side, and then rolled up into a ball as he vainly struggled to fill his lungs with oxygen. Edgar stepped in behind the Headmaster, awaiting orders.

Jonah reached down the back of his pants and stuffed the note between his buttocks. The last push was uncomfortable but necessary. He knew what was coming next.

"I said," the Headmaster grabbed Charlie by his beard and dragged him to his knees, "what were you doing?"

"Free study—we were practicing reading words like you told us," Jonah muttered quickly.

"Search them," the Headmaster said to Edgar, ignoring the lie. He let go of Charlie's beard and walked in front of Jonah, staring into the inmate's eyes with less than six inches of space between their noses.

Edgar grabbed Charlie by his neck and pinned him against the wall. Charlie's knees buckled when Edgar began his search, but he somehow maintained his posture.

"Jonah, what really happened?" the Headmaster asked menacingly.

"Richard is the only one that reads good, so he was reading out loud to us first," he blurted. "That's what really happened."

Headmaster Green nodded sarcastically, pretending to sympathize. "I see, but unfortunately the book is facedown, so you weren't reading, were you?" He pointed to the book and looked from Jonah to Barry with accusing eyes.

"Richard did it," Barry said quickly.

Richard, confused, raised his hand, as if classroom rules somehow applied. Headmaster Green drove his heavy fist into Richard's midsection, near the center of the skinny prisoner's diaphragm, knocking the wind out of him and making him crumple to the ground.

"Books are not toys. I've told you several times—" Headmaster Green kneed Jonah in the groin, doubling him over and sending him to the floor alongside Richard "—to not place books face down like that. When you're done reading, you put them back on the shelf where they belong."

Barry, the last one standing, watched Edgar drag Richard to his feet and throw him against the wall, where he initiated a thorough search of the prisoner's uniform. Headmaster Green shook pain from his hand and strolled over to Barry, who began to shiver with fear the closer he got.

"Don't piss yourself," the Headmaster warned. Barry shook his head frantically, refuting the very idea.

"Good; now Barry, can you please put the book back on the shelf?" Barry quickly nodded and stared back at the Headmaster, whose anger was building with each passing second. When he finally realized what had been asked of him, Barry hurriedly picked up the book and jammed it onto the shelf upside-down, his hands shaking throughout the process. He spun back to the Headmaster, his swollen lips smiling with pride. Headmaster Green smiled back, but his face suddenly darkened as he punched Barry in the side of his midsection, crushing his freshly broken ribs, making him collapse in anguish.

Edgar found nothing on Charlie or Richard. Jonah was surprised and grateful that Edgar avoided his posterior entirely during the search. Barry couldn't stand up straight, so Edgar searched him on the floor. Mitch hadn't woken up since the beginning of class, but he was searched anyway. Eventually, they were released back to their cells, leaving the Headmaster and Edgar empty-handed.

Jonah limped inside his cell and leaned against the feeding table until the door closed. He could hear the sound of Edgar locking Richard's cell door and then his heavy boots walking away. He dug into his buttocks, retrieved the note, and then looked around for disposal options. He sniffed the paper and instantly gave up on the idea of eating it, like he had done with the other note.

Pained and wincing, he knelt down, unlatched the hatch of his excretion duct, and opened it. He looked into the darkness, unable to see anything but dim light reflecting off standing water, and tossed the balled-up paper through the duct.

As he shut the hatch cover, he heard something splashing slowly through the unseen expanse below him, but that was nothing new. Something was always moving around down there.

CHAPTER 7

And so the routine of Cydonia 6 endured. Some days were better than others; time slowly passed, the seasons gradually changed, and the calendar inched through its 687-day cycle. Inmates exercised, sat through classroom lessons, and kept eating their assigned foods—whether they liked it or not.

Charlie ate lamb, while his opposite number 21, Arva, ate carrots; Richard ate celery, while Sue, also numbered 22, ate poultry; the 23's (Barry and Beth) consumed beef and peppers, respectively; the 24's (Jonah and Edith) ate broccoli and venison; and of course, Mitch continued to be force-fed onions.

As far as the men knew, female 20 was still missing. Her shutters hadn't been opened since being closed the night of the feast, just after her marriage to Mitch. But the female prisoners knew the truth, even Edith. They had all heard the stories from Arva; Carol was being held captive in her cell.

Except for Hilda and Dr. Selleck, Arva was the only one in camp who had actually seen Carol since the feast. Her cell was just across the hallway from Arva's, so every time Carol's door opened, Arva sneaked a look through the notch in her door. But even then, she could only see one of Carol's wrists and one of her ankles, both of which were shackled to the wall of her cell by thick metal chains.

***

SEPTEMBER 12, 2335 M.E.
3:36 PM

Hilda walked into Carol's cell holding a plate of fatty pork and closed the door behind her, shutting out Arva's prying eyes. "Feeding time," the scarred enforcer said grimly as she approached the shackled inmate.

Carol's number patch was covered in dried vomit, as were her neck and chest. But the extremely pregnant prisoner was genuinely happy to see Hilda, the only consistent human contact she had. Hilda hadn't beaten her since the lump in her belly had started to grow, so Carol naively assumed that they were now friends.

Carol did her best to sit up, but her chained hands and feet, and her large belly, made it difficult. "Is it winter yet?" she asked excitedly.

Hilda ignored her. "You're not going to throw up again, are you?" she asked warily, an implied threat lying in wait behind her tone.

Carol's smile vanished, and she quickly shook her cleanly shaven head, fearing that the unspoken truce between them was about to be broken. "I won't, I promise!"

"Good," Hilda cooed, making Carol relax. "If you eat the whole plate, I'll give you an orange pill."

Carol's wide smile indicated that she was on board with the plan. Ever since her marriage, her orange pill count had been greatly reduced. She greedily consumed the pork as Hilda fed it to her, and then paused, her mouth still full. "Hilda?"

Hilda held the fork up to Carol's mouth, doing her best not to engage her on anything beyond the food. She knew that free thought and self-analysis had no place in the Cydonia camps, especially by the staff, but adherence to that ethos was becoming increasingly more difficult as lots were liquidated.

"How long 'til I'm cured?" Carol asked innocently.

Hilda looked coldly at the baby bulge and then back into the prisoner's eyes. "Dr. Selleck said two weeks."

Carol tentatively accepted another bite of pork as a dark fear crept into her mind. "It's been moving a lot, like something… alive is inside me."

Hilda gritted her teeth, choked back emotion, and fed Carol another bite of discolored pork. "You'll be cured soon—don't worry." Her fake, nearly invisible smile made Carol brighten considerably. She gladly stuffed her mouth with the pork, swallowing it down in hefty chunks.

Hilda silently scraped another portion together, her thoughts turning to the worst of her memories: the war, killing, constantly struggling to survive, and of course, her own near-death. Even though the rancid tusk of one of the Pale Giants had pierced her neck, millimeters from her jugular vein, she had still managed to force a bayonet through its jack-o'-lantern-sized eye before it could finish her off.

Yes, things could be much, much worse.

* * *

3:45 P.M.

Jonah didn't know that the tall, rugged, sinewy black man who was looming over him had been dishonorably discharged from the GCMC for malpractice. As with all the other staff members, the doctor's background was a complete mystery.

At one time, Dr. Selleck had been a highly skilled battlefield surgeon with a stellar reputation. But after he botched an operation and killed a patient while high on opiates, his military career was ruined. In the doctor's defense, he had just needed something to numb the reality of seeing all that blood every day.

After his conviction and dishonorable discharge, he had two

options: stay and get rich, or go back home in disgrace; the choice was easy to make.

To Jonah, Dr. Selleck was a kind, understanding man who stitched him back together after beatings, cured his illnesses, and cared about things he said. The doctor was the only member of the staff that Jonah felt he could trust.

Dr. Selleck poured cold water over Jonah's head, rinsing the remnants of lice shampoo into a large bucket. "OK, all done." He reached for the stiff, scratchy, over-bleached towel reserved for inmates and draped it over Jonah's head.

Jonah smiled and rubbed his long hair with the towel. "Those little bugs itch."

"Hope we got all of them," Dr. Selleck said, mildly concerned.

Jonah finished scrubbing his scalp and held out the towel to the doctor, who refused it and pointed to the ground. Jonah tossed it to the appointed spot and sat back up in the only chair with a cushion that he had ever sat on. "Did you get in trouble for cutting Richard's hair?" he asked with a smirk.

"Little bit." Dr. Selleck smiled back at him, withholding the full explanation. He walked to the sink and washed his rubber-glove-covered hands with soap. Even though it was unhygienic, expensive latex meant that gloves had to be used until they fell apart.

"Have you ever seen your face, like in a picture or glass?" Dr. Selleck asked offhandedly.

The question baffled Jonah. "Glass?"

"Windows? Never mind."

Jonah searched his memory as he thought about the doctor's first question. "At the transition camp I saw my face in a bunch of grass water once. My head hair was shorter, and I didn't have face hair, so I could see what I looked like, kind of," he added.

Dr. Selleck unlocked and opened the medicine cabinet, retrieving syringes filled with colored fluid from within. "What else do you remember about the transition camp?"

"Headmaster McGinnis, my friends, lots of other people I didn't know, and that gross paste we all had to eat."

"You like it better there or here at Cydonia 6?" The doctor sat on a stool fitted with small wheels and rolled next to Jonah, who mindlessly hiked up his sleeve.

The doctor emptied the first syringe—a battery of steroids, growth hormones, and protein—into Jonah's shoulder while the inmate stalled for time. He could read hesitation all over Jonah's face. "You know, I never tell anyone what we talk about, including the Headmaster." He retracted the syringe and swabbed the entry point with a cotton ball. "Do you tell anyone?"

"I never do, not even Barry. You're the only one I talk to about stuff."

"Good." He prepared another syringe, this one a dose of vitamins and minerals, and stuck Jonah in the shoulder again. "I'm curious about something. How come you and your friends never try to escape?"

Confusion over the inanity of Dr. Selleck's question twisted Jonah's face. "The guards, they're in the towers and the forest all around here. If I broke out, they'd kill me!" he said forcefully.

Dr. Selleck removed the syringe and swabbed Jonah's skin. "Pretend for a second there were no guards. Would you escape?"

"I don't know," Jonah replied, stumped. "I'd really miss the pills."

"You like pills that much?"

"I do!" Jonah said quickly, smiling at the mere thought of orange pills. "What's in them, do you know?"

Dr. Selleck nodded. "Vitamins, steroids, growth hormones, fertility drugs sometimes, and lots and lots of narcotics."

Jonah smiled. "I don't know what any of that means."

"They're full of things that make you grow, keep you healthy; also things that make you want to stay here instead of escaping."

Jonah nodded, pretending to understand. "Oh, OK. Why does everyone get different kinds, though?"

The doctor carefully placed the empty syringes on the steel tray and retrieved the third and final syringe, a dark green solution of condensed broccoli extract laced with a light dose of heroin. "You've been eating broccoli for almost three years now, since the day you arrived. You're a little over six years old now, so that's about half your life."

"Tell me about it." Jonah had a vague memory of the first few times he had eaten broccoli, when he actually enjoyed the taste.

Dr. Selleck injected Jonah with the green syringe. "Since you only eat broccoli, your body needs other things to keep it running. Pills and injections give you those missing things."

"But Barry gets four brown pills; I get none."

"He only eats beef, so his body needs different kinds of the missing things to keep it running. That's why he gets brown pills and you don't."

The explanation sunk in. Jonah was impressed. "You explain words good."

"Thanks."

"What does the word 'mon-ster' mean?" Jonah asked quizzically.

Dr. Selleck froze, the reference sending spikes of ice through his veins. "I don't know that word," he lied robotically.

Jonah leaned forward and lowered his voice. "I read it on a note that—"

"Time to go," Dr. Selleck said sternly. He rolled the stool back, stood up, and placed the third syringe next to the others. Just like his rubber gloves, the syringes would be cleaned and reused. He turned the faucet on and placed the syringes in the water basin, rinsing each in purified water.

Jonah, heavily confused over the doctor's reaction to his question, got up from the chair and carefully exited the office. After the door shut, Dr. Selleck turned the faucet off, closed his eyes, and leaned against the counter. He couldn't bring himself to even try to explain what the word meant. If he did, Jonah would never willingly go back into his cell.

CHAPTER 8

Through swollen eyes, Mitch glanced bitterly from the female barracks, where Hilda was closing the window shutters, to the four male inmates clustered near the Lines of Division. The others had no idea how different things were for him now. Every hour spent without *her* was an hour wasted.

He was taken aback by the intense feelings that had arisen between him and Carol, his opposite number, after they were sequestered in the marriage hut for seven days and seven nights. They bonded in more ways than he could have imagined, and talked about anything and everything on their minds; just being with her opened his eyes to a whole new world. After those experiences, going back to the mindless reality of daily routine, including not speaking to Carol anymore, was a horrifying idea. He wanted out, and to be with her, like the Headmaster had promised; but he was still there, and no one had seen Carol since the feast.

He still clung to a dwindling hope that the two of them would be released from camp soon, but this optimistic perspective was eroding at an ever-quickening pace. Dr. Selleck kept shaving his head every week, and from what the doctor said, that was a sign that his time as an inmate of Cydonia 6 was about to end. Problem was, he didn't want to be released on his own. Carol needed to be by his side, just as the two of them planned, so that they could take the first steps into freedom together.

***

5:57 P.M.

Jonah shivered under his burlap blanket and searched the yard for Mitch. He was tired of listening to Charlie tell the same stories about the old days in camp, and for the first time in a long time, Mitch was conscious enough to have a conversation. Mitch stood alone in the southwest corner of the yard, about twenty yards from the fence. Jonah broke off from the other three inmates and trudged over to the taller man, whose eyes were fixed on the women's barracks.

"Feeling better?" he asked hopefully.

After a prolonged silence, Mitch replied, "No."

"Thinking about what you're doing when you get out of camp?"

"Thinking about Carol," the lanky inmate said with a whimper.

"What?" It was a word he had never heard before.

Mitch stared at the female barracks. "Shared everything with her."

Jonah understood now, he was talking about female 20. "What's her food again?"

"Pork." The memory of it made Mitch smile. "So good," he said enthusiastically.

Drool dribbled out of Jonah's mouth. "Pork... I'm eating two plates of that at the next feast," he said, salivating over the mental image.

"You still haven't seen her in the yard?"

Mitch had asked him the same question thirty minutes ago, but since he had been the subject of many beatings recently, being forgetful was understandable. Jonah shook his head, which made Mitch droop with sadness and worry.

"She left already, without me." His lip quivered as he held back tears.

"No, you would have left too," Jonah reassured him. "Married couples always leave together."

Mitch's bruised face hardened. "Did Charlie ever tell you what happened to Female 19?"

"Yeah, she left the day they got married, left him behind." Jonah had heard the story more times than he could count. Charlie loved talking about how the world had wronged him.

Mitch shook his head. "She escaped through the excretion duct in the marriage hut."

Jonah refused to let the words sink in. "She didn't leave, Mitch. Female 20's just sick or something."

"Carol," Mitch said coldly.

"Carol," Jonah agreed vacantly, mentally sidetracked by Mitch's version of what happened to female 19.

"Charlie's been eating lamb for nine years, Jonah. I'm not eating onions that long!" Mitch's trembling voice cracked.

"They won't bump you up. You're leaving with female… Carol really soon—that's that." He shook Mitch gently, attempting to comfort him.

The thought of leaving hand in hand with Carol made Mitch brighten. His swollen lips curled into a smile. "We did this thing where we took our clothes off and touched our mouths together," Mitch said excitedly. Jonah's brow furrowed as he thought through the mechanics of such an awkward act. "And something else that felt *great*," Mitch stressed emphatically.

"What did you do?"

"It's hard to describe; the feeling was…" Mitch rubbed his shaved chin.

"Like orange pills?" Jonah suggested hopefully.

"Not really," he dismissed.

A deep, rolling grumble resounded through the cool evening

air, just beyond the gravel road, drawing their attention to the murky shadows and dense overgrowth of the forest. Something was out there, and it was close, but neither man was alarmed. They were behind the fence, which was supposedly an impregnable barrier; to them, animals were nothing more than a curiosity.

A handful of instances, both Mitch and Richard had seen glimpses of animals wandering the forest, with each sighting occurring on the cusp of nighttime, when shutters were being closed. Jonah's only experience seeing an animal was months ago, but that was during the day. He kept his eyes trained on the shrubs bordering the gravel road, hoping that he would get a good look at the mysterious creature, but it was also important to keep Mitch's spirits up.

The taller inmate's growing insolence about camp rules had begun to affect the others, and Jonah was tired of getting beaten just because Mitch wanted to cause trouble. "Which way are you going when you get out? Do you know?" He quickly glanced at Mitch, who was also fixated on the forest, and then turned back, unwilling to miss one second of animal-observation time.

"Where the sun sets—more light that way," Mitch said absently. Sounds of snapping twigs and heavy breathing were approaching from due west. The animal, whatever it was, was coming closer to camp.

A Pale Giant suddenly pushed aside tree branches with its wide arms, forcing its way out of the gloomy foliage and into the waning sunlight. Its large, deformed head drooped to one side, two spear-length tusks jutted out from its misshapen mouth, and its bare, ghostly pale chest was marred with scars of melted skin. Mitch and Jonah stared raptly at the beast, exhilarated by its presence.

It sniffed the air while licking its brown teeth with a thick, gray tongue. Bulbous eyes examined the two inmates staring back at it; it grunted defiantly, then ducked back into the shadows just as quickly as it had appeared. As sounds of the Giant's retreat began to dissipate, Jonah and Mitch regained their breath.

"You ever seen an animal before?" Mitch asked in a crisp, lucid tone.

"Yeah, me and Charlie saw one in the morning, the same day that really clean man with the crazy clothes was here."

"I've never seen one up close like that. It was looking at us." Mitch, deep in thought, tightened his burlap blanket around his shoulders and slowly walked away, leaving Jonah alone at the fence.

Slightly unnerved and needing distraction, Jonah regarded the huddle of inmates standing near the Lines of Division. His thoughts rotated to a familiar subject, one that would surely take his mind off the animal and how scary it looked: inmate politics.

Mitch's revelation of female 19's escape needed to be thrown in Charlie's face. He had been telling them a lie for years, a fact that both intrigued and annoyed him. Charlie must have more information to share; Jonah decided that he would drag it out of him. He plodded across the patchy grass, passing Edgar, who was closing the shutters to the men's barracks. He arrived at the Lines of Division just as Barry said something that made Richard and Charlie laugh.

"What happened to female 19?" Jonah demanded.

Charlie cast a dark look at Mitch, who was roaming the yard alone near the south fence, figuring the taller inmate had betrayed his confidence. "I told you already, she left after we got married, the day after the feast."

"How did she leave?"

Richard and Barry both turned accusingly to Charlie, suddenly very interested in his pending response. Charlie gulped; he was cornered. "She left—does it matter how?"

"Through the excretion duct, in the marriage hut?" Jonah vented angrily.

"She escaped?" Barry said, flabbergasted. "Why didn't you tell us before?"

"You've told the story a million times; why not tell us the end part?" Richard jeered, piling on, his half-bald lips pursing as he awaited a reply.

Charlie glared at them defensively. "I'm not talking about it. They already bumped me up twice!" He stormed off toward the barracks and pulled his burlap blanket tightly around himself, sulking.

A single horn blast from the guard towers reminded everyone in camp that men's exercise was over. Mitch wandered in from self-imposed isolation and joined the slowly forming group of men that was lining up next to the barracks entrance. Edgar opened the door, and the five thin prisoners shuffled inside. Although Jonah wanted to tell the others, even Charlie, about seeing the animal, he would have to save it until the cells were locked and Edgar was gone. The last horn of the night meant silence.

Charlie stared at Mitch's closely trimmed head as the lanky younger inmate walked quietly into his cell. Half of Charlie hated Mitch for spilling the beans; the other half was relieved that the secret was exposed. At least now he could talk about it and share the memory with the others.

Edgar locked Mitch's cell and then Charlie's cell, as Richard, Jonah, and Barry walked to their cells. Richard fearfully turned back to Jonah, whose eyes darted past the younger man's oddly shaved face and head, and to the light coming from cell number 24.

Jonah stopped in the hallway, letting Barry pass, too afraid to take another step forward. A sharp jab from Edgar's baton got him moving down the hallway again. Jonah shuffled into his cell, cowering with fear, his gaze frozen on the stained, ruddy floorboards.

Barry and Richard stared curiously through their notches as Edgar entered the cell behind Jonah and shut the door.

Jonah stood in place and trembled as he awaited attack from the sweaty, stinking presence now lurking behind him. He ventured a quick look toward his feeding table and found two shiny shoes that he recognized instantly. As his head slowly tilted up from the shoes, his eyes met the furious face of Headmaster Green.

The Headmaster sat at Jonah's feeding table, a twin of Edgar's baton in his hand. "Good evening," he said flatly.

Being spoken to meant he could speak. "What did I do?" Jonah blurted.

"You tell me."

Jonah realized that he had a long list of things he could admit to doing, "I don't know." Edgar swung his baton in a downward arc against Jonah's spine, sending a shockwave through his body and making him collapse to the ground.

Headmaster Green stood up, looming over him. "Say the first rule of Cydonia."

"We only eat assigned foods," Jonah croaked as red hot agony spread across his back.

"And you've been eating paper?" the Headmaster leaned on his knees, looking Jonah squarely in the eyes. "Paper?" he roared, and clubbed Jonah's shoulder with his baton, almost dislocating bone from socket.

"You only eat assigned foods," Headmaster Green said tritely.

"I'm sorry," Jonah sobbed.

The Headmaster angrily beat Jonah's thighs, and then his ribs, making the prisoner curl into a pathetic ball of pain. Breathing heavily, the Headmaster slicked his hair back and sat down on the feeding table. "This time it's one night in the hole." He grabbed Jonah's hair and lifted his head up. "If I ever have to talk to you about your diet again, I'm taking away your orange pills, permanently. Do you understand?"

"I won't do it again, I promise," he groaned.

Edgar withdrew the sedative syringe from his apron, lowered it to Jonah's arm, and paused. He looked at the needle's contents and then shamefully turned to Headmaster Green. "It's only a quarter dose."

"Good, he'll be lucid enough to eat. Make sure he has an extra serving of broccoli before you put him in." Headmaster Green kicked Jonah. "And you'll eat all of it, right?"

"All of it, Headmaster," Jonah groveled. Edgar emptied the syringe into his arm and hauled him to his feet. Jonah limped as Edgar dragged him out of the cell, down the hall and out into the yard.

The sun was low on the horizon and the orange sky was slowly turning red. Although his shoulder, ribs, and thighs were bruised, Jonah liked being outside in the hole once in a while. He usually got a big shot of orange bliss and could lie down in a new environment for the night.

Edgar stopped and straightened Jonah's slouch into a stand with a violent yank to the back of his neck. "Don't move or I'll beat you 'til you can't move at all," he ordered. Jonah wobbled on his feet as he felt the injection numbing his body. With drooping eyes, he watched Edgar stride to the south fence, unlock the gate, and disappear into the administration area.

A shrill scream from the female barracks suddenly sliced through the narcotics overwhelming his mind, drawing his curious eyes to the rickety structure on the other side of the Lines of Division. Grunts and muted sounds of pain followed the scream; Jonah could only assume that it was a beating. From what Charlie said, Hilda was just as hot-tempered as Edgar.

Drugs engulfed Jonah's senses, and his head tilted back, his eyelids almost closing. High in the sky he could see distant flecks of twinkling light. He didn't know if they were stars, but they were beautiful all the same.

The south fence gate squeaked; Edgar returned to the yard holding a plate full of cold, overcooked broccoli. He handed the plate to Jonah, who accepted it with two hands, making sure that he didn't drop it, especially in his stupefied state.

"Eat it all, right now, or I use the stick." Edgar twirled the baton in his hand.

Wasting no time, Jonah chomped on the broccoli, stuffing it in his mouth. Another distant scream emanated from the women's barracks, making him look across the yard again. Edgar produced a full syringe from his apron and held it up in the fading light, verifying the dosage. He jabbed Jonah in the side of his damaged shoulder with the needle, through his uniform, making him wince.

The mild sting ebbed instantly, a robust stream of opioids obliterating any semblance of sensation. Jonah looked back into the sky as he crammed a sickly broccoli stem into his mouth. The moon emerged from behind wispy clouds, brightening the yard and the surrounding forest. "Eyes on your food," Edgar grumbled, and withdrew the syringe from Jonah's arm.

Jonah shoveled the last of the broccoli into his mouth, and with cheeks full, he licked the plate clean. Edgar yanked the plate out of his hands and examined it. "Good enough—in the hole."

Jonah stumbled into the long, grave-like ditch and curled into the fetal position, his mind systematically shutting down. Edgar dropped the warped plank of wood over the hole and rolled the heavy stone on top, pinning Jonah underneath. Before Edgar finished dusting his hands off, Jonah was asleep.

* * *

6:00 P.M.

Headmaster Green slowly fixed his tie as he walked down the hallway of the men's barracks, his thoughts distant and dark. The Masters had somehow known that Jonah had eaten paper but refused to give him any background on the discovery. Paper was scarce. The most recent shipment was years ago, just before the last lot of products had been liquidated, and that was just two packs of notepads. He would have to check the classroom books for torn pages.

"Headmaster?" a hopeful, weary voice asked.

Headmaster Green stopped and smiled to himself. He hadn't heard that tone from Mitch for quite some time. Maybe the smart-mouthed bastard had finally learned his place. Although he had just broken the rule of silence, Mitch had been taking a lot of punishment lately; this one time, and only if Mitch kissed his ass, he would let it slide. He strolled slowly to Mitch's cell door, where he found eyes looking at him through the door notch. "Yes?"

"I wanted to ask about female 20. Did she leave already? I'm worried about her."

Headmaster Green's brow wrinkled in confusion. Sometimes he forgot how mundane and pathetic reality was for the inmates. "There's no reason to worry; she's just been sick. Hilda tells me she's doing much better now," he said phonily, silently laughing to himself.

Mitch breathed out with relief. Headmaster Green leaned forward and smiled. "You'll be together very soon, I promise."

CHAPTER 9

Arva nervously paced the ancient planks that lined the floor of her cell, biting her nails and wiping away tears of anxiety as wood creaked under her steps. The screams now coming from the cell across the hallway weren't as loud as they had been a couple of hours ago, but they sounded much worse, as if Carol were being tortured.

Dr. Selleck had visited Carol's cell earlier in the day, but he stayed for only a few minutes before hurrying out. The doctor was the only staff member that seemed to care about the well-being of the prisoners, so his sudden appearance, and even quicker exit, worried Arva to no end. *Why had he come? Why did he leave? Carol needs his help!* The words echoed through her scrambled mind as more screams shook the barracks.

Arva sat at her feeding table, leaned on her elbows, and then sat back up. She didn't know what to do with herself. Nearby, a plate piled high with cold, limp carrots awaited consumption. She knew the longer she waited to eat them, the worse they would taste, but none of that mattered tonight.

"You need to push now, ready?" Hilda's voice sounded oddly positive, as if she were conveying sympathy. Arva got up from the table, propped herself against the door, and stood on her toes. She peered through the narrow horizontal window, hoping to catch a glimpse of something, anything, in the hallway. She couldn't see inside Carol's cell, but she could at least hear both of them clearly.

"Push!" Hilda's loud instruction was followed by sounds of strained agony, as if Carol were being crushed to death.

Arva walked to the wall she shared with Beth and lowered her eye to a hole that was once a large knot in the wood. Rumor had it that one of the former inhabitants of the barracks stole a fork and used it to carve a hole in the wall. Apparently, she passed the fork to another prisoner, as the wall that Beth shared with Edith had a similar hole in it. Arva and Beth used it to talk to each other; Edith used the hole in her wall to spy on Beth.

Beth paced in front of her door, beside herself with worry. "Hilda's killing Carol!" she said in a loud whisper. Moans and heavy breathing from Carol's cell suddenly became loud, strained screaming.

Arva chewed on her fingernails. "Maybe she's pulling that big lump out of her belly."

Beth tersely smacked her lips. "Carol hasn't left her cell in four months, and now Hilda is helping her?"

"It hasn't been that long."

"Right after she got back from the marriage hut she got sick. Maybe male 20 gave her a bacteria, like Dr. Selleck talks about."

The very idea terrified Arva. She was next in line to get married; catching a bacteria from a man could kill her. "She was only with him seven days. How could she get so sick?" Arva argued, doing more to convince herself than Beth that getting married had nothing to do with the illness.

Across the hall, Carol's grunts of pained exertion reached a crescendo, and a new sound pierced the air, the wails of a newborn baby. "You did it!" Hilda proudly exclaimed.

Arva dashed back to the notch in her cell door and looked

through it, desperately searching for the source of the crying and wailing.

"It's beautiful! It was in me the whole time!" Carol's voice was joyous; Arva smiled to herself.

"Shhh, we don't want the others to know, OK?" Hilda scolded.

"Can I hold it?"

"No," the word was spoken icily, in the familiar tone that Hilda usually used with Arva and the other inmates.

"Don't take it away!" Carol screamed, near tears. Carol's begging was suddenly cut off by three muffled popping sounds.

"What was that?" Arva heard Beth ask through the wall. Beth could barely see Carol's cell door through her notch, so every detail had to be conveyed second-hand. Arva ignored the question, not wanting to forgo one second of concentration.

Carol's cell door swung open, revealing Hilda, who immediately met Arva's stunned gaze. The female enforcer cradled a crying baby in her arms, a nest of plastic wrap bundled around it. Her right arm was splattered with blood; her hand held some kind of metal device that was also stained with blood. Hilda's scarred face instantly transformed from a look of guilt back into her usual hardened jail-keeper expression as she stormed off down the hallway, clutching the crying infant.

Arva turned to the hole in the wall, where Beth's right eye peered through. "It was a little person!" she said, both baffled and excited. She turned and looked through the notch in her cell door again, hoping to find something that explained what she had seen. Now that Carol's cell door was wedged open, she could see almost everything in the mysterious room across the hallway.

Arva's blood instantaneously froze as a macabre image met her eyes. The event taking place in the cell across the hall didn't look real, and didn't make any sense. Carol's body was being dragged through her excretion duct by an unseen force, her body barely fitting through the small square that was cut into the floor of the cell. Her head and arms were already through, leaving only bloody feet and legs, and the remnants of her burlap uniform. Carol's listless feet disappeared through the duct, leaving behind a thick streak of blood.

Shock gripped Arva's chest, making speech impossible.

"Arva?" Beth asked, concerned over Arva's sudden change of expression. Arva slowly walked away from the door and over to her excretion duct, trembling as she slowly got to her knees. "What are you doing?" Beth demanded incredulously.

Arva reached back to hold her hair in place and lowered her head, being careful not to touch the sides of the square hole as her face passed through the opening. The excretion duct was a place she normally kept her nose away from at all costs, but she needed to see what was going on below.

She heard a heavy object being dragged through liquid and odd breathing sounds. The loud splashes and guttural grunts quickly moved away from her duct and deeper into the dark. With trembling hands, Arva shut her excretion duct and closed the flimsy hasp, her sense of security smashed into a thousand pieces. "Beth, shut your duct and lock it."

"Why?" Beth demanded.

Arva gulped, her mind racing at the thought of trying to explain what she had seen—and heard.

* * *

6:49 P.M.

Hilda hurried toward the gate at the south fence, fighting the urge to console the small, premature baby crying in her arms. Tears streaked down her face as she unscrewed the silencer from the end of her pistol while balancing the baby in the crook of her arm.

Too much blood; she'd fucked up, should have taken a few steps back before firing. It had been quite some time since she murdered anyone, but that was no excuse. A lot of water would have to be wasted to clean up the mess. She turned her attention to the sky, finding a purple canvas twinkling with distant stars, and picked up her pace. Being outside after sundown was dangerous. Doing so with fresh blood all over you—while holding a crying baby—was suicide.

Hilda reached the south fence and stopped suddenly in her tracks. The gate had already been unlocked; she could feel someone, or something, watching her.

Edgar stepped out from the shadows on the other side of the fence and swung the gate open, his face void of emotion. "You going to make it?" he asked indifferently.

Hilda pretended to be offended. "I'm delivering it, aren't I?"

"Where's the product?"

"They… already took her." Her voice shook but steadied at the end.

Edgar nodded, instantly seeing through her pretense. The once-beautiful, now scarred and battle-hardened female enforcer had been softened by life in camp. Edgar remembered the days when Hilda would have shot him in the face for questioning her loyalty.

"I took care of mine, you take care of yours." Hilda walked away defiantly into the maze of sidewalks that was the administration area, leaving Edgar alone at the gate.

Unlike Hilda, Edgar looked forward to the task assigned to him this night. He'd wanted to do it months ago, but the female went and got herself pregnant, and the bonus would only be paid if the man, woman, and baby were served at the same time. The amount of gold coming his way as a result made it well worth the wait. He walked quickly toward the men's barracks, crossing the Lines of Division while loading his silenced pistol. Old habits made him keep his eyes up and at attention. He scanned the trees and the space beyond the surrounding fence, finding movement in multiple places. The crying baby had riled them up; he tied his long, greasy hair back and broke into a jog.

He unlocked the barracks entrance, stepped inside, and quickly shut the door behind him. He could hear one of the Pale Giants moving through the line of trees just beyond the gravel. Even though the sun was still barely in the sky, the very sight of them scared him down to the bone.

He breathed out, relieved, and turned left into the hallway; it took only six steps to reach the door of Mitch's cell. Edgar carefully unlocked the door, quietly swung it open, and stepped two paces inside. Luckily, Mitch's light was off.

The sudden influx of light from the hallway woke Mitch from a deep sleep, and a dream about walking through the forest with Carol. He rubbed his eyes, his burlap blanket sliding to the ground as he slowly sat up. "Carol?"

* * *

6:54 P.M.

Charlie had heard someone enter the barracks but was too scared to look through the notch in his door to investigate. Seconds ago, two bright flashes and sharp yet muffled noises had come from Mitch's cell. Good or bad, he wanted no part of changes to routine. He closed his eyes and told himself that he was sleeping and this was a dream—even the heavy thump and dragging noises that were happening in the hallway—all a dream.

* * *

6:56 P.M.

Edgar cracked the door open and surveyed the darkness outside. The Giant was gone; he had to get this over with quickly. He dragged Mitch's corpse into the yard behind the barracks, dumped it, and then ran back to lock the front door. One bullet in Mitch's neck, and another in his chest, had caused catastrophic blood loss, and the smell of blood meant a lot of interest from *them*.

A fading glow above the trees indicated that nighttime was imminent, and being outside at night was against the rules. He wrapped the chain around the door's metal handles, clicked the lock shut, and then ran at top speed back to Mitch, where he picked up his legs. Sweat poured down Edgar's temples as he dragged Mitch's body across the yard. Scraping sounds from the perimeter fence meant that one of them was on the gravel; reluctantly, and without losing a step, he looked.

It was a Giant, an albino mountain of extraterrestrial muscle that resembled an ogre or titan from ancient legends. It walked parallel to the fence, tracing Edgar's progress through the yard while sniffing the air. Steam poured out of its mouth, with tendrils of heated air dissipating as wisps around its menacing tusks; long claws dug into the gravel as it brachiated alongside the fence; blood was in the air, and the sun was almost down.

The Giants were a silent third party to the Truce of Cydonia, an agreement that had settled a century-long war and paved the way for the Cydonia camps to be built. Although the enormous monsters didn't speak, they obeyed the rules as strictly as the humans and Masters. Violation of the Truce by any of the three species meant that all bets were off, and Edgar knew how violent the Giants could get—it was like fighting an elephant-sized rhino bare-handed.

Huffing and puffing, he jogged toward the south fence gate with Mitch's legs pinned under his armpits, forcing himself not to look back. The last shard of sunlight vanished behind the trees as Mitch's corpse crossed the threshold into the administration building.

Edgar breathed heavily as he trudged up the hallway to the Headmaster's office; a ragged trail of blood streaked across the floor behind him. Shrieks from the newborn baby echoed through every corner of the building. He dragged the body inside the office, where he found both Headmaster Green and Hilda. He dropped Mitch's legs and leaned against the desk, slowly regaining his composure.

"Perfect timing," Headmaster Green said in his phony voice, the one he always used when he was nervous. "We were just concluding business regarding the bonus."

Hilda handed the crying baby, still bundled in plastic, to two long, black, scaly arms that were sticking out from the hatch in the floor. The Master's claws stunk like rotten meat and feces, making her dry-heave. The tall Master didn't like the light in the Headmaster's office, but she could still see its glowing red eyes, sharp fangs, and thick snout in the darkness below. The Master turned the baby over to another one of its kind, who was hidden somewhere in the basement, and then stuck its foul-smelling, clawed hands up the hatch again. "Onionsss," it hissed.

Edgar rolled Mitch's body to the hatch and backed up as the Master's scaly, insect-like arms quickly collected the corpse and dragged it down into the depths below.

Headmaster Green shut the hatch and fastened the six steel bolts that secured the sturdy wooden panel to the floor. He looked up at Edgar and Hilda and smiled. "Well, my friends, we're rich."

CHAPTER 10

Barry burped while gnawing on a wad of fatty beef. He was halfway through feeding and he already wanted to stop and just eat pills, but he knew better. After orange pills, he wasn't even close to being hungry, and today Edgar gave him two oranges instead of one.

A screech of feedback echoed from the guard tower, signaling that an announcement was imminent. Barry stopped chewing and turned toward his window.

"Attention, inmates, this is your Headmaster. I have good news. Although the feast was tentatively scheduled for two weeks from now, it will commence at dawn tomorrow instead." Barry couldn't believe his ears. He smiled widely and continued chewing. "There has also been a change in the marriage order."

Now Barry wanted to vomit; a change?

* * *

Richard rocked back and forth as he crammed celery into his mouth, excited at the idea of eating all sorts of things, all day tomorrow. He scratched his stubbly skull, fantasizing about the various foods he would consume as he swallowed a mushy clump of celery. Although he liked his new haircut, the tiny hairs that were growing back really made his head itch.

"Number 21, lamb and carrots, have been bumped up to Number 25. Therefore Number 22, poultry and celery, will be married tomorrow instead." Celery mush dribbled down Richard's half-shaved chin, his astonished mouth hanging agape.

"That will be all," the Headmaster's voice concluded happily.

* * *

Jonah, having just regained consciousness, wasn't sure if he was dreaming or not. Dim light showed through a crack in the plank above him. He was freezing his balls off, just like every time he slept in the hole for the night, so it appeared the news was genuine. Even though he was beaten up and crammed into an uncomfortably small ditch, he managed a smile. The feast was tomorrow! He would eat everything but broccoli.

* * *

Kill myself. The words echoed in Charlie's grief-stricken mind, over and over, long after he stopped crying. But he didn't know how to snuff out his own life. Even if he did, he probably wouldn't go through with it because he was a coward.

The best thing to do, he decided as new tears welled up in the corners of his eyes, was to fight. He couldn't just keep hating the world and eating lamb. It was time to do something about his situation. It was time to escape.

CHAPTER 11

Barry and Richard hovered at the Lines of Division, uneasily monitoring Charlie, who had wandered off to the north fence just after Edgar let them out into the yard. Charlie stood slouched over and unmoving at the same spot he had been standing earlier in the day, during morning exercise. Even after the worst of arguments and/or beatings from Edgar, Charlie would have been talking to the others by now. But he hadn't said a word since the announcement.

"Bumped up three times," Barry shook his head sympathetically. "He's got to be mad."

"Yeah, it's not good," Richard said hollowly. "For him," he quickly corrected. "For me it's good." He couldn't hold back a smile any longer. He was getting married tomorrow!

"What do you think he'll do?" Barry nodded toward Charlie, ignoring the bait. They had talked about Richard's impending marriage all damn morning, and he was sick of it. Plus, something was really, really wrong with Charlie.

"He'll still eat lamb; he's just number 25 now. He gets married after Jonah," Richard said, annoyed. Barry should have known all of this already. "Already gave him a new patch."

Charlie heard Richard's words distantly; he looked down at his chest, finding the freshly added number 25 patch sewn into his uniform. Unfamiliar emotions stirred inside him again, feelings and thoughts that had first crept into his consciousness as he watched Edgar sew the patch on during morning feeding. He was determined to find a way to stop eating lamb, or at least die trying.

Barry and Richard turned toward the sound of the south fence gate opening. Edgar walked through the gate and over to the hole, where he rolled back the large stone that secured the wooden plank to the ground.

"I wonder if Jonah told about the writing," Barry said.

"Didn't hear him say anything," Richard mumbled.

"Neither did I; I share a wall with him, remember?" Barry spat, irritated. "I meant outside, with Edgar."

"We'll find out soon enough." Richard slowly walked along the Lines toward the hole, with Barry following closely behind.

Edgar lifted the plank covering the hole, and dropped it aside. He reached in with one hand, grabbed a knot of uniform collar, hauled Jonah out, and dumped him unceremoniously on the ground.

Jonah got to his knees and then pushed himself up to a shaky stand as Edgar exited the yard through the south fence gate. He stretched, yawned, and trudged toward the other two prisoners, his mind and body numb from an opioid hangover and a thorough baton clubbing.

"Did you tell?" Barry asked excitedly.

Jonah shook his head. "Headmaster thought I was just eating paper." He nervously scanned the yard, making sure that no authority figure was within earshot. "I heard some really weird noises out here last night," he said carefully.

"Talking?" Richard volunteered energetically, clumps of dirty hair flopping over onto the clean-shaved half of his head as it swiveled between the two men. "About the feast tomorrow, maybe?" Barry rolled his eyes.

"No." Jonah's mind was still emerging from a fog, but he knew it wasn't talking. Richard's face drooped.

"Did you see Mitch?" Barry asked, quickly changing the subject. "His cell was empty this morning."

"I think Edgar took him inside last night," Jonah nodded to the administration area. "That's what I was talking about, the noises. It was Edgar breathing, but breathing really hard, like after he beats us and he's tired. Like this," Jonah quickly breathed in and out to mimic what he had heard, but the sudden change in his oxygen level, and the fact that he was still swimming out of a drugged haze, made him stagger and nearly pass out.

Barry steadied Jonah, who leaned on him for support. After the yard around him stopped wobbling and his eyes refocused, he looked toward the north fence and the pathetic figure standing hunched over next to it. "Is Charlie OK?"

"He's not talking to us," Richard said, perturbed.

"I think he's not talking to *Richard*," Barry amended.

Jonah suddenly remembered the big news. "So, tomorrow, huh?"

Richard beamed. "Yeah, I can't wait!" he said loudly. Barry waved his hand, indicating that Richard should lower his voice. "Oh, right, sorry," Richard said in a hushed tone. "I can't wait to talk to the female. I've been thinking of things to say all morning, like… what doesn't she like about poultry? And… what color pills she likes best."

Barry nudged Jonah, and they both looked at Charlie, who now had his fingers wrapped around the chain-link fence.

"You think that's enough things to say?" Richard asked to the back of their heads. "Guys?"

"Yeah," Jonah replied vacantly. Suddenly, Charlie violently tugged on the fence, as if trying to tear a hole in it with his bare hands. The other inmates bolted toward him, with Jonah arriving last.

"Stop it!" Barry wrapped himself around Charlie's from behind, and the older, withered man collapsed against him, sobbing.

"The guards would catch you," Richard scolded, "and hands on the fence is forbidden anyway, didn't you—"

"Shut up, Richard!" Charlie shouted, spittle flying, as Barry slowly released him.

Charlie's anger melted into anguish. "I can't remember anything before the transition camp. I've been standing here, trying to, but I can't. Not one thing." Charlie turned and looked out through the fence, into the forest. He had been watching the world go by through a fence his entire life.

"Should have gone with her," he said wistfully. "But I was scared. We had just gotten married. She wanted me to go, but I didn't," he whispered regretfully.

"Your turn will come," Barry encouraged.

Charlie looked at the others with red and hateful eyes. "You've only been here for three years. Nine years I've been here!" He glared at Barry. "I don't even know if I have a turn anymore."

CHAPTER 12

Headmaster Green stood next to the blackboard, holding a long pointer made of blue plastic. To him, teaching the idiot inmates was the most annoying phase of their development protocol, but scientists back home claimed that increasing their intellect quickened body growth. The only advantage to the classroom that he could see was that it kept them busy and (mostly) out of trouble.

"I know you've heard this lesson before, but in light of tomorrow's event, it bears repeating." He pointed to the words "rules of the feast," scrawled in dull chalk on the blackboard. Three other words were written below them: "females," "food," and "wine."

"Today, we'll be reviewing the rules of the feast," he said, bored, and pointed to the word "females." "No interaction will be done with the females, except Richard—"

Richard sat up straight, smiling ear to ear. His head, lip, jaw, and chin were cleanly shaven. With all the hair gone, Richard's head resembled a pale kernel of uncooked popcorn.

"—who will be sitting on the blanket in the gray zone, in the middle of the Lines of Division. The rest of you will be seated, or standing, an appropriate distance from the Lines."

Even though they had gone over the same information months before this lot's first feast, where the out-processing of male and female 20 began, Headmaster Green could tell they didn't understand everything he was saying. As long as they didn't fuck anything up for him, he didn't really care if they understood or not.

He pointed to "food" with the blue pointer. "Your favorite topic!" he said, intentionally mocking their pathetic existence. "You will be allowed as much food and wine as you want, and also allowed to not eat your assigned foods for one whole day. We'll have bread, cheese, meat, and of course scrumptious wine." Headmaster Green tapped the last word on the list with his pointer.

Barry's arm shot into the air. "What's scrum-pum… tious mean, Headmaster?" he asked tentatively, trying to remember how the word had been pronounced.

Headmaster Green absently swatted Barry's hand with the pointer, making him painfully withdraw. "Now, if you get a little tipsy or sleepy from the wine, that's perfectly normal. You'll just wake up in your beds safe and sound the next morning."

He put the pointer down and leaned against the desk, surveying the faces of the inmates. All but Charlie were paying rapt attention. "Now, before we leave, let's all say the rules of Cydonia." Charlie hadn't moved, which was very unusual. He was typically the quickest of the group to obey commands; Headmaster Green made sure to keep his eyes squarely on the gray-haired inmate, unsure of how the next few minutes would unfold. "The first rule is?"

"We only eat assigned foods," Jonah, Barry, and Richard said in disjointed unison. Charlie's eyes stared off as his lips mouthed the words.

"Right—except for tomorrow. Second rule?" He got up and strolled to the southeastern corner of the room, putting himself directly in Charlie's line of sight. The inmate's unfocused eyes slowly blinked. He turned to the front of the class, maintaining a martyr's slouch while passively avoiding any interaction, both verbal and nonverbal.

"Females are numbers, not names," Jonah, Barry, and Richard droned. Charlie vacantly mouthed the words again.

"Excellent," Headmaster Green said as he strolled toward the west wall of the classroom, hands in his pockets. "They are only numbers, even when alone—Richard—in the marriage hut." He circled back around the inmates as if a vulture analyzing carrion, slowly retracing his steps.

"The last rule," he said as he casually leaned on his desk.

"We close the shutters at night," three inmates responded. Charlie didn't even bother mouthing the words this time.

"Correct; are there any questions before you go?" His eyes burned through Charlie's skull, knowing what was coming. Charlie's small, pale hand shook with tremors as he raised it into the air. Finally, he looked at Headmaster Green. "How did I know you had a question, Charlie?" the Headmaster quizzed sarcastically.

"Why did you bump me up again?" The words dribbled out, barely avoiding the tone of a whimper. "I'm twelve now," he squeaked.

"What?" the Headmaster shouted, pretending to not hear him.

"I said I'm twelve now, twelve years old."

"So?" Headmaster Green's hands curled into two fists.

"I want to leave, but you bumped me up again. Why?"

Jonah exchanged worried glances with Barry as Headmaster Green pushed himself away from his desk, moving closer to Charlie, and then leaned down, crossing a personal-space threshold that made Charlie cower.

"We've talked about this twice before; Dr. Selleck has told you countless times. Your special age isn't right for your special marriage," he said through a wicked smile. He leaned in closer, snarling lips now inches away from Charlie's stinking rat's nest of a head. "Did I finally answer that question for you?"

"Are you going to bump me up again?" Charlie asked after an extended silence.

"And what if I do?" the Headmaster responded with hateful malice. Charlie crumbled into a ball and sobbed into his folded arms.

Headmaster Green, proud of himself, got up and checked his watch. "OK, gentlemen, we'll call it quits a little early today—dismissed." He adjusted his suit jacket by the lapels and strode out of the class, leaving Jonah, Barry, and Richard to console an inconsolable Charlie.

The instant the door shut, Headmaster Green's mind turned to more important matters. Anxiety fluttered in his chest as he walked quickly through the hallway and unlocked his office door. In the war, he had killed them, sometimes from the air, sometimes from a distance with a rifle, other times with his bare hands. Now, he managed their restaurant.

He pushed his desk back from the large, square hatch door cut into the floor and disengaged six steel bolts from their sturdy hasps. As the hatch swung upward, the foul stench of decay and bodily waste flooded his nostrils.

Headmaster Green looked into the small mirror on his desk and practiced the smile he used when dealing with them; which one of them was always a guess. He hoped it was the smart, thin, businesslike Master with a spotted snout, and not the hostile, aggressive one with excessively long fangs.

He stepped down through the open hatch and onto the ladder that led below. As he descended, the smell got worse, so bad that it affected his eyes. Holding back vomit, Headmaster Green eventually reached the bottom, and strode onto a muddy, squishy surface made of God knew what. Reeking water flooded his shoes and soaked his legs to a level just above his ankles. At least the flooded basement was shallow today; during the last meeting, the rotten sewage was up to his waist.

Light from the office above illuminated the basement in a narrow column; he sheltered his eyes with his hand and scanned the darkness. He heard it before he saw it. A low-pitched purr echoed, and then unseen steps splashed toward him. A tall silhouette emerged from the shadows and stared down at Headmaster Green with glowing red eyes.

It was a Master unfamiliar to him, a young, thin one with spindly arms and legs. It looked basically the same as the rest of the hideous creatures, but with slimmer shoulders and a fatter snout riddled with green spots. As with every single one of them he had ever seen, gelatinous drool dripped from its sharp fangs.

Headmaster Green implemented his rehearsed smile. He saw something glittering in one of its long, scaly hands, so he was going to play nice from the get-go. "Master, I need to report that male 25, lamb, is behaving unusually. I think he's planning escape."

The Master let out a long, disapproving groan and chomped its teeth, making spittle fly into the murky water. "I've tried the usual. Beatings, the hole, more opiates, but he's not responding. The last change to the schedule seems to have affected him more than we could have imagined."

"Lamb must be aged," it said in a booming voice that drenched the air with a vulgar smell. "The special bo-nussss will pay when we say prepare the dissssh." The Masters learned English in hours and read books in minutes, but most of them struggled with spoken language. Their mouths and tongues simply weren't capable of replicating the sounds that humans made.

"Of course," Headmaster Green replied smarmily. "I hope order 20 came out well?"

"Yesssss. Onionsssss, pork, delicioussss," it purred.

"And dessert?"

"Fressssh and alive, for now."

"Wonderful," the Headmaster beamed pretentiously. He could tell that the creature was done conversing from its brevity.

It dropped a heavy, bloodstained burlap sack full of gold nuggets by the Headmaster's submerged feet, its scaly hands momentarily visible in the light pouring down from the office above. Long, discolored claws were still wet with liquid blood; the Headmaster must have just interrupted its meal.

Headmaster Green crouched and searched the foul-smelling water with one hand, rescuing a few gold nuggets from the disgusting, yogurt-like silt while holding the sack upright with his other hand. It would be tough getting the heavy bag of valuable metal up the ladder, but the struggle would be a pleasure.

The Master took a step forward, closer to the light, and tilted its deformed head downward. For a moment, Headmaster Green thought he was a goner. His eyes slowly rotated up from the sack of gold and looked directly into the wide red eyes of a gruesome monster.

"Prepare the disssssh, order 22, poultry and celery. Bo-nussss pay for each live dessssert. Half bo-nussss pay for each dead," it hissed.

Headmaster Green's practiced smile returned. "Agreed." They were getting a taste for newborns, which might be a problem down the road. For now, there wasn't any harm in getting filthy rich off of the inmates' offspring.

"The new lot that followssss order 25; will you extend the contract?" it asked while its serpentine tongue licked specks of human flesh from its fangs.

"It will be my honor, Master." The tall creature turned toward the darkness and the subterranean maze that spread out below the prison camp. "But," Headmaster Green quickly added; the Master turned and looked over its shoulder. "I need to ask for a small, five percent increase to the fee."

Its breathing quickened, and its teeth chomped disapprovingly as it turned and faced the Headmaster once again. "Our Governor visited; he's getting greedy," he blurted nervously, "threatened closure of the camp if I don't pay more. The Giants liquidated camp 11, so we have to spread out costs—that's the reason he gave me, at least."

"Greedy," the skeptical tone of the word was followed by a deep purr.

"He's a politician—I'm sure you understand." Headmaster Green initially doubted himself after saying it, but then he remembered how incredibly knowledgeable they were of human culture and customs. Of course it knew what a politician was. As it stared him down, the Headmaster realized how vulnerable he was at the moment, standing alone, unarmed, in its territory.

"Agreed," it finally said, and departed quickly into the darkness.

Headmaster Green let go of a lungful of nervous breath as heavy steps and splashes faded. He squatted down next to the bag of gold, wrapped both arms around it, and tried to stand up, but the weight was too much. He would need the winch and cable this time; he smiled as he ascended the ladder. If female 22 had twins, he would need a forklift to get the gold out.

CHAPTER 13

Unusual sounds roused Jonah from a dream about eating bread, a wonderfully soft, edible substance he had tasted only once before, at the feast when Mitch got married. He breathed out, angry, and rolled over. The dream was just getting good. He desperately hoped it would pick up right where it left off, whenever he fell back asleep.

As his mind slowly drifted back to unconsciousness, hollow, distant sounds of splashes and bumps echoed beneath the floorboards of his cell. He sat upright in his bed and listened to the darkness; he could also hear heavy, frantic breathing. Jonah turned toward his open excretion duct, the source of the commotion, confused over what he was hearing. As the sounds continued, he hopped off of his thin wooden bed and clicked on the small lightbulb just above it. He slinked over to the duct, where he crouched down and turned his ear to the opening.

He stuck his head through the duct, searching for the cause of the noises. After his eyes adjusted to the darkness of the basement, Jonah could only see dim light reflecting off of water. The awful smells of the subterranean maze below made his nose wrinkle.

"Shit! Shit! Where's the... shit!" a familiar, tearful voice rife with panic was coming from somewhere in the depths below.

"Charlie?" Jonah could not comprehend the idea that Charlie, of all people, was running around in the basement, especially at this time of night.

"Jonah?" Charlie shrieked gratefully. "Where are you?"

Jonah put his arm through the duct and waved at the darkness. He saw something moving around but wasn't sure if it was Charlie. "I'm here! Where are you?" Charlie abruptly appeared in the light, his face, hands, and uniform covered in wet mud. He held his right leg, unable to put weight on it.

"How did you get down there?" Jonah asked, astonished that Charlie had found enough courage within himself to risk escaping.

"I climbed through my duct, then fell and hurt my leg, then I tried to get back up but I couldn't," he babbled. "Then I..."

"Reach up!" Jonah interrupted, and extended his arm down as far as it could go. Charlie reached for Jonah's hand, standing on his tiptoes, but their fingers remained a good distance apart. "Jump up!"

"I can't!" Charlie whined. "My leg hurts too much."

A low-pitched purr suddenly reverberated off the walls of the basement, and a tall silhouette moved through the darkened expanse. The air coming from below now smelled extra rotten.

"Something's... down here, Jonah." The gray-haired inmate's head swiveled as he searched the shadows. He looked back up, his eyes gleaming from fresh tears. Jonah would never forget how Charlie's eyes looked in that moment.

"I think it's a—" Charlie let out a chilling scream that was instantly cut off as he was swept away by a scaly blur.

Jonah lingered at the duct, fearing the worst for his old friend. "Charlie!" A loud snapping sound cut sharply through the foul air, followed by low-pitched grunts and wet, crunching noises. "Charlie!" Jonah shouted again through the square hole.

Something splashed through the darkness, quickly getting

closer to Jonah's duct and the beam of light that poured through the opening. Jonah saw a tall outline traipsing through the water, each step making a wide wave as it fell, and then its eyes—two glowing red orbs as large as Jonah's hand. Whatever it was, it wasn't Charlie.

Jonah hurriedly closed the wooden hatch and secured the duct with its rickety slide bolt, then dashed to his lightbulb and clicked it off. He dove onto his bed, faced the wall, and pulled the burlap blanket up under his chin.

Mysterious thumps resounded from below his cell. Jonah's heart walloped against the inside of his chest as he hoped against hope that the sounds would magically go away. A louder thump pounded against his excretion duct hatch, making his anxiety level shoot through the roof. Jonah pulled his blanket over his head; something wanted in. Another blow against the duct hatch destroyed the slide bolt and made the wooden square explode upward, where it crashed against the wall under his feeding table. Jonah shivered as adrenaline overtook his nervous system.

He heard something clamor through the open hatch and up into his cell; it was heavy, and reeked of decomposing meat. Boards creaked as it stepped towards Jonah. The helpless inmate mentally withdrew into himself, shutting down as many connections to his body as possible. He didn't want to look and see what it was, the thing that was currently sniffing his burlap blanket; if he did, he might die from the shock.

Sounds of inhalation and a tongue flicking against deformed fangs moved from Jonah's feet to his head. From the sound of it, it liked what it smelled. Time vanished as Jonah succumbed to the need to tune out reality. It was breathing in his ear now. When slimy drool fell on his cheek, the physical world shut off.

CHAPTER 14

Barry leaned against the wall of the hallway and yawned, while curiously looking at the empty space to his right, a section of floorboards upon which Charlie should be standing. Edgar had collected Charlie's plate, but he hadn't unlocked and opened the older prisoner's door.

Edgar bent and retrieved Jonah's plate, then unlocked the cell, holding his baton up and ready throughout the process. Barry scrunched his face up, confused. For unknown reasons, Edgar was being excessively careful with opening Jonah's door. Something was amiss, but Barry didn't care what it was, as long as it didn't prevent him from getting to the food.

Last night, bad dreams about people yelling in the basement had kept him up all night. If it weren't for the feast today, Barry would have begged Edgar to let him get more sleep.

Edgar swung Jonah's door inward and was surprised to find him standing by the feeding table. The excretion duct hatch lay broken on the floor, ripped off at the hasp. Wide, oddly shaped footprints made of dried slime and claw marks led from the hatch to Jonah's bed plank.

Jonah wobbled on his feet, his eyes swollen with sleep deprivation. Edgar breathed out, slowly relaxing. He nodded at the windows, choosing to ignore the trail of footprints on the floor. "OK, move," he instructed, and Jonah shambled to his window to unlock the shutters.

Jonah's mind was numbed by terror and tiredness; his fingers moved robotically over the shutter lock until it was open. He was shocked that Edgar hadn't beaten him for the broken duct cover, but there were more pressing things to worry about. He had endured an eternity the previous night, waiting for the foul-smelling creature that had hovered inches above his face to attack him. It had made all sorts of weird sounds while sniffing and looming over him, as if deliberating over what to do next. Hours and hours had passed before Jonah finally worked up the courage to turn and look to see if it was still in his cell, but it had disappeared through the duct.

Jonah trudged out of his cell and lined up behind Barry, near the barracks door. Barry acknowledged him with a polite nod as Richard exited his cell. Jonah desperately needed to tell both of them the events of the previous night, but he might not have a chance until after the feast. By then, Richard would be in the marriage hut with female 22, and Barry would be asleep.

Richard beamed with happiness as he fell in line behind Jonah, his smile stretching ear to ear. He rubbed his hands greedily; he couldn't wait to get outside. Although Jonah was still emotionally drained and shaken to his core, he managed a grim smile. He wanted to be happy for Richard, but he couldn't now. Not after last night.

"Hey, did you guys hear weird stuff in the basement last night?" Richard asked innocently.

Jonah's eyes opened wide and his lips barely held back an answer. He looked at his feet as Edgar walked past him.

"Kinda," Barry said sleepily. "I was dreaming, though, I'm…"

Edgar opened the barracks door, letting dreary sunlight and fantastic smells wash across the inmates. The aromas immediately silenced Barry and drew the prisoners' attention to the outside. The feast was no longer a fantasy waiting to be realized. Barry eagerly led the other two inmates out into the yard, where the morning air was crisp and the grass chilly with frost.

Jonah marched around the corner of the barracks and immediately looked across the Lines of Division to the women's side, where he found the four female inmates. Hilda was herding them toward the center of the Lines, upon which a large gray blanket had been placed.

As female 25 met Jonah's wide eyes, her beauty knocked the wind out of him. Seeing her up close and in person like this made him want to reach across the Lines and touch her, just once, to verify that she felt just as good as she looked.

The other inmates, both male and female, were fixated on two tables overflowing with food that sat on either side of the Lines, near the north fence. Each table was set up approximately ten feet from the black and white plastic divider.

Headmaster Green strolled lazily along the Lines of Division as both sets of inmates converged on the gray blanket and sat down on the grass in semicircles behind it. He gritted his teeth as he thought through his approach to the upcoming conversation with the Masters. All hell had broken loose since last night's escape attempt. With a litany of problems to fix, he had no time to waste playing make-believe with the inmates.

Richard and Sue stared at each other across the gray blanket with awkward, wide smiles; their heads were so cleanly shaven that they reflected sunlight. Barry and Beth, the 23s, also maintained eye contact, as did Jonah and Arva. Arva smiled, her eyes twinkling. Jonah's heart thudded in his chest as he clumsily smiled back. Edith shot hateful daggers through Arva's head with jealous eyes.

"I know you're eager to get to the food, but I do have a quick announcement," Headmaster Green lectured, his attention going back and forth between the two groups of inmates.

"Male number 25 was released early last night, for good behavior. We gave him a pair of magic slippers, which are things that cover your feet, like shoes," he explained, motioning to his own feet, "and he wished himself away. Isn't that wonderful?"

Barry's hand shot up into the sky as he bit his lip; he rocked back and forth excitedly, barely able to contain an outburst of inquiry. "No questions!" Headmaster Green snapped. Barry's hand reluctantly fell back into his lap.

"Now it's time for male and female 22 to come forward and be seated in the gray zone," Headmaster Green pointed to the center of the blanket. Richard and Sue stood up, tentatively walked onto the blanket, and sat in the middle of it, only a few feet apart. Two metal plates and two dirty cups lay between them.

"Male and female number 22, as your Headmaster, I officially confirm your marriage," he said grandly. "Starting now, you will spend seven days and seven nights together, where you will share everything, including a bed, assigned foods, and even conversation."

Richard gulped, excitement overloading his body. His hands shook; his tongue was caught in the back of his throat. Sue struggled to hold back joyful tears. Headmaster Green bent down and touched Richard's and Sue's shoulders. "Congratulations, you two."

Edgar and Hilda removed foil and plastic wrap from their respective tables, revealing bountiful mountains of food. "OK, everyone, you may eat!" Headmaster Green announced.

The inmates stormed toward the tables in a mad rush. Richard slowed as he approached the men's food table, smiling as Barry and Jonah jockeyed in line next to it. The person getting married always went first, so he was going to milk the privilege, just like Mitch had months earlier.

The three male prisoners stared at the food. Deli meats, cheeses, slices of bread, and bowls of jam and butter sat alongside a buffet of assigned foods—pork, lamb, poultry, beef, venison, onions, carrots, celery, peppers, and broccoli.

Richard salivated as he hovered over the table, using his free hand to gather food and stuff it on his plate, taking one of every-thing—except celery, a substance he would be avoiding for the next seven days. He stuck his fingers into the butter and gouged out a scoop, then did the same to a bowl of jam. After grabbing a jug of wine, he hurried back toward the gray blanket, sucking on his sticky fingers, tasting an ecstasy of flavors.

Barry and Jonah, meanwhile, attacked the food table at a furious pace. Barry took a handful of cheese and crammed it into his mouth as he filled his plate. Jonah focused on the meats and heaped one of each kind on his plate. He looked across the Lines of Division and found female 25 slowly stacking sliced bread onto her plate. As she turned away from the table, her eyes darted to Jonah and then quickly looked away. She shook her head briefly and then sat down on the grass behind Sue, knowing that Hilda and the Headmaster were both watching her closely.

Jonah knew what the gesture meant. It was a reminder of the message he had found in the spine of the history book: don't eat or drink at the feast. He looked down at the pile of food he had col-lected, unsure of how to proceed.

Headmaster Green walked behind the men's food table as Barry shoved more cheese into his mouth. Jonah quickly walked away from the table and sat in the grass behind Richard. Suspicious eyes tracked every step. Barry sat down next to Jonah, his mouth still full of cheese, and opened a jug of wine. He sloppily filled his cup and Jonah's, then hurried back to eating.

Jonah sneaked a look at Arva and found her picking at a bread crust. She turned her cup, showing Jonah that it was empty, and then tipped it back and pretended to drink from it. With shaking hands, Jonah avoided the meats overflowing from his plate and picked up a piece of bread. He followed Arva's example and munched on the crust of the bread.

Resisting the urge to shove handfuls of meat into his mouth

got much harder as Barry and Richard tore into their food. Jonah stealthily dumped his cup of wine into the grass and then tipped back the empty cup as if drinking from it. Apparently, he had done a terrible job of hiding his actions because Barry saw everything.

"What's wrong with the wine?" Barry said, bits of cheese and poultry spewing from his mouth. He shoved an entire chicken breast into his mouth, making his cheeks bulge.

"Shhh!" Jonah admonished, confusing Barry even more, and took another small bite of bread. Drool spilled out from the corners of his mouth as he crunched on the crust. Barry was taken aback, but now was not the time to worry about it. The two men had no secrets between them. If Jonah wasn't eating, there had to be a good reason.

The two bald inmates sitting on the gray blanket were quickly filling up with food, their voracious pace slowed to the point that they were looking at one another again, instead of staring at their plates. Richard felt nervous sweat bead on his freshly shaven head. He wanted to say something to her; after all, he had been practicing conversation topics since yesterday. He opened his mouth; Sue stopped chewing, her eyes intently watching him, waiting for his first words to her. Richard's mind froze, unable to process something to say. He shoved beef into his mouth and sheepishly looked away. "Hi," he said, mumbling to his plate. Eventually he worked up the courage to look at her.

Embarrassed, and knowing it was her turn, she managed a quiet reply. "Hi," she said, and smiled through a mouth half full of food.

Richard was pleased that the ice had been broken, but what now?

"What's your food?" Sue asked, forcing her voice to hold confidence.

"Celery."

"Mine's poultry."

"I know," Richard said sarcastically, making Sue uncomfortable.

"Celery's gross," he blurted, hoping the admission would get their conversation back on track.

"Poultry's gross," she said sweetly, and they shared a small laugh.

Headmaster Green appeared beside them and squatted down. "I see you're getting along nicely." He picked up their jug of wine and shook it. "You haven't had any wine yet? Here, I'll pour you some." He opened the jug and filled their crude cups, then stared at the two prisoners until they drank. "Now remember, no touching in public, or you'll be beaten with the baton," he reminded pleasantly.

"We know, from what happened at Mitch's…" Richard trailed off, suddenly realizing that he had spoken the name of a male inmate in front of a female, which was a blatant violation of the rules. "At male 20's marriage," he corrected, pretending, and failing, to nonchalantly shrug off his gaffe.

Headmaster Green smiled, letting the transgression go. "So if you touch each other, you'll know why you're being beaten, won't you, male 22?"

"Yes, Headmaster," Richard nodded quickly.

Satisfied with Richard's subservient tone, Headmaster Green walked over to the female food table, where he stood next to Hilda.

Arva had been monitoring the Headmaster and Hilda in her peripheral vision ever since sitting down on the grass. She needed them to engage in conversation, or better yet, turn their backs to her, so they wouldn't see her breaking the rules.

Hilda leaned against the women's food table, jostling it; an empty food container slid to the edge of the table, nearly falling off, but Headmaster Green reached and saved it from falling at the last moment. During those three seconds of commotion, Arva quickly dumped the contents of her plate onto Beth's plate. Although none of the staff witnessed the exchange, one of the inmates saw everything.

Edith's buck teeth poked through her lips as a wicked smile widened across her homely face. Throwing away food was forbidden, and this time she wasn't going to let Arva get away with misbehaving. Hopefully, Headmaster Green and Hilda would beat her right here.

The hunched-over, oddly-shaped girl got up from her isolated spot in the grass and shuffled toward the female food table, where the Headmaster and Hilda stood. Along the way she peered at Jonah, who ignored her. His attention was locked on her enemy. Telling on Arva had just become a little easier.

She arrived at the table, holding her empty plate, and stared at Headmaster Green until his attention was on her.

"Enjoying the food, female 24?" he asked as if speaking to a child.

"Headmaster?" Edith asked carefully.

"Yes?"

"I just saw something."

* * *

8:36 A.M.

Barry was finishing his second plate of food when he noticed Jonah nibbling on bread, the pile of meat on his plate left untouched. "You're not eating anything else?" he asked, mortified.

Jonah scanned for authority figures and found Edgar standing behind the men's food table, and Headmaster Green and Hilda talking to female 24 at the women's table. "Charlie didn't get magic slippers, Barry. I saw something take him, from below us in the basement, something big. It was the mon-sters, I think, like what the writing said."

"You saw it?" Adrenaline pumped through Barry's veins. He always wondered what was making all those noises in the basement.

"I didn't just see it. It came up through my excretion duct, into my cell!" Jonah said loudly, his hushed tone disintegrating as memories of the moment flooded back.

Richard turned around, quizzically examining Jonah; Jonah faced his plate again, realizing that other people could hear. In no way, shape, or form did Jonah want Headmaster Green knowing about the incident with Charlie and the mon-ster.

"Why aren't you eating, though?" Barry's one-track mind got back on the rails. Food was everything to him. Well, food and pills.

"The writing said so: don't eat or drink at the feast!" he hissed as quietly as possible. "If there's mon-sters, the rest of the writing is true too!" Barry's inability to absorb the basics really pissed Jonah off sometimes.

"Forget the writing and the mon-sters! Two whole years we went without a feast, and before that, we only had paste, remember?"

Jonah did remember, and he knew he was taking a huge risk based only on the scribbled handwriting of a former inmate, but he didn't care. Female 25 was doing it, so he was going to do it too. "I want to see what happens."

Barry rendered judgment on Jonah's decision with a look of disgust. "You're dumb then." He resumed stuffing his face but made sure to show Jonah what he was eating before scooping up the last bits of cheese.

Barry licked his plate clean as Jonah looked down at his own plate, which was bulging with food. "You won't tell, will you?" Jonah's desire to withstand the urge to eat was crumbling.

Barry pretended to think it over. "No," he finally said, and smiled. "But you have to tell me what happens."

Jonah breathed out, relieved. "I will."

"OK, give me your food, then." Barry had been looking at the poultry leg on Jonah's plate since they sat down. Jonah put his plate on the grass and reached for Barry's. "Wait," Barry said, and Jonah froze. "Not the beef. I'm not eating that."

Jonah nodded, halfway happy. There was only one way around this. He picked up the thick slice of beef and shoved it into his mouth, the buttery material seemingly falling apart with the first bite. His eyes rolled back into his skull as the taste trickled down into his stomach. "You eat this every day?" he asked, in ecstasy.

"It's not that good, trust me." Barry picked up Jonah's plate and shoved the meaty end of the poultry leg into his mouth.

Jonah swallowed the last mouthful of beef and reluctantly retrieved Barry's empty plate from the grass. He grabbed his cup, got up, and quickly walked toward the men's food table. He had to get away from Barry, or else he would rip the plate out of Barry's hand and tear into the rest of the food himself. He held back drool, savoring the remnants of the taste of beef. It would have to be water and bread from here on out.

Jonah avoided Edgar's eyes as he piled slices of bread onto his plate and filled his cup with dirty water. Headmaster Green crossed the Lines of Division and nodded to Edgar, signaling him to clear out. Edgar quickly obliged.

The Headmaster sidled up next to Jonah, who had been acting suspiciously since walking into the yard this morning. After what he had just heard, there could be a serious problem brewing. He didn't want to liquidate the lot, not now. Starting over with a new set of ten inmates would take forever and would cost a shitload of money. "Male 24, enjoying the feast?"

"Yeah." Jonah turned to look at the Headmaster, then glanced at Edith, who stared back at him as she walked along the Lines of Division, holding a plate overflowing with food.

"Don't let me stop you—dig in!" Headmaster Green waved his hand grandly over the food.

Jonah felt slobber well up from under his tongue; he wanted to, so badly. "I have… bread, Headmaster," he finished meekly, and showed Headmaster Green his plate.

"Well OK then," Headmaster Green said sarcastically.

Jonah began to leave, but Headmaster Green stopped him with a firm hand on his shoulder. "Male 24?" he asked sweetly, as if addressing a puppy. "Almost forgot your wine." Headmaster Green confiscated Jonah's cup, threw out the water, and filled it with wine from a jug on the table. He stepped in closely, looking the stinking inmate directly in his frightened eyes, and handed him the cup.

"Thanks," Jonah said, his voice quivering, "the wine's really good." He scuttled off, nearly running, and sat back down next to Barry.

Headmaster Green put the jug of wine back on the men's food table and wiped his hands on a napkin. He knew Jonah too well: the food would be excruciatingly hard for him to resist.

An internal alarm went off, and he checked his watch. The meeting with the Masters was in less than ten minutes, and he never wanted to be late to a fee delivery. Hopefully Charlie's aged lamb taste pleased them; then maybe the fee wouldn't be reduced too much for early delivery. He fixed his tie and crossed the female half of the yard, walking quickly through the south fence gate and into the administration area.

* * *

3:50 P.M.

As hours dragged by, the inmates ate, drank, and frequented their respective barracks to relieve themselves. Edgar and Hilda doled out a midday ration of pills to the inmates, and the mood of the feast shifted from excitement to relaxation.

Jonah curiously saw a change in Barry, Richard, and the female inmates within an hour from pills being distributed. Everyone but female 25 and Jonah was wobbly and slurring their speech.

Jonah and female 25 had continued their silent connection via eye contact throughout the day, both sticking strictly to bread and water. They were waiting for something, although neither was sure for what exactly, but at least they were doing it together.

By the time the sun began to sink in the sky, the inmates were intoxicated. Richard and Sue laughed together, Beth and Arva were virtually attached at the hip (just like Jonah and Barry), and Edith sat isolated in her own sector of grass.

"I still want to know why they took my orange pill and then gave it back. I love those ones," Barry slurred drunkenly as he ate butter off of his finger. "I miss them if them don't give... them to us." He slurped purple jam from his plate.

Jonah rolled his eyes. Barry was barely making any sense, and he was becoming more regretful of not partaking in the feast with each passing minute. Nothing had happened yet, and he was tired of waiting.

Barry licked his plate clean and laid back on the grass, his knees sticking up into the air. "I wonder what Mitch is doing?" he asked lucidly, then yawned.

Jonah thought back to Charlie being taken, which made him fear the worst for Mitch. "He said they were walking toward the setting sun," he said vacantly.

"Walking and no fence; that sounds too good to be true," Barry opined, and yawned again, adjusting his position and extending his legs to maximize comfort. "Out in the woods, though, animals... no pills... that would be rough." Barry slowly shut his eyes.

Jonah saw Richard lying on his stomach, quietly talking to female 22, who was also prone. Conversation, in general, dimmed as the prisoners gradually passed out, one by one. Edgar and Hilda were next to the food tables, seated on plastic chairs taken from the classroom, surveying the group of inmates; they too seemed to be waiting for something.

Female 25 smiled at Jonah as she curled up on the grass. She shook her head quickly, and then closed her eyes. Jonah understood; he would pretend to fall asleep too. He stretched out and shut his eyes.

Eventually, he heard sounds of someone walking through grass, and slightly cracked his eyelids open. Hilda was walking among the female inmates, carefully examining each one. That meant Edgar was probably doing the same thing to the men. Jonah snapped his eyes shut and relaxed his jaw as heavy steps walked up behind him. He heard Edgar's labored breathing and felt a nearby presence, but both quickly vanished. He sneaked another look and found Edgar meeting Hilda on the gray blanket in the middle of the Lines of Division.

Edgar picked up female 22 by the armpits, as Hilda picked up her lower legs. They walked her unconscious body over to the south fence, where they laid her in the grass next to the gate. They walked back to the blanket, picked Richard up, and hauled him over to the fence, where they set him down next to female 22.

Hilda unlocked the gate and swung it open as Edgar maintained his grip on Richard's armpits. She hoisted the limp prisoner up by his ankles and walked backward, leading them through the gate and into the administration area. Jonah guessed he was being taken to the marriage hut, where he would spend the next seven days alongside female 22. The marriage experience had ruined Mitch. He hoped things turned out much better for Richard.

Jonah let his eyes fully open. There was no way that Edgar or Hilda could see him now, but he didn't dare move. After a few minutes, the two enforcers returned and collected female 22, and then Hilda locked the gate. More time passed, and the yard quieted. Jonah began to hear odd sounds coming from the administration area, where Headmaster Green, Edgar, Dr. Selleck, and Hilda lived: laughing.

Grass rustled and he raised his head. For a moment, he feared it was the thing that had clawed its way up through his excretion duct last night, but instead he found female 25 crawling on her belly to the Lines of Division. Jonah gulped down anxiety, rolled to his stomach, and crept toward her. She was looking right at him; no authority figures were in sight, and everyone else was asleep. He knew what was coming next.

"I'm Arva," she said in loud whisper, and smiled. They were very close to each other now, with only the Lines of Division separating them.

"Jonah," he replied robotically, and forced a smile. He was petrified but wouldn't ruin the opportunity. "What… what color pill do you like best?" He would have to thank Richard later for providing some material in his hour of need.

Arva shook her head, her face scrunched up in disbelief. "Forget that! You saw the writing hidden in the book, from number 16?"

"Yes," he nodded slowly. "I saw something else too. A monster took Charlie, male 25, in the barracks basement. It climbed up through my excretion duct, into my cell." Jonah was shocked that Arva was taking the news so well.

"It took Carol, female 20, and dragged her through the duct." Jonah looked away, absorbing the information. "We can't stay here; the monsters will take us too," she said softly.

"Wait, you say it like *monsters*, not mon-sters?"

"Yes, Jonah!" Arva retorted sarcastically.

He liked hearing her say his name, just like he was happy to know hers, but it was hard to face the reality of what she was articulating. "Female 19 escaped through the excretion duct in the marriage hut. Charlie told me," he said numbly, knowing that Arva would want to act on the option.

"How did she get away from the monsters?"

Jonah scanned his memory for the missing information. He had heard the story from Charlie countless times: Charlie had awakened the day after the feast to an empty marriage hut, and he never saw female 19 again. It was only recently that Jonah learned she had gotten out through the basement. "Charlie never said."

"We need to try," she said, her eyes twinkling, mesmerizing him.

Booming laughter from the administration area made Jonah and Arva instantly pretend to be asleep. Jonah cracked his eyes open and saw Edgar take a swig from a bottle as he stumbled along the concrete sidewalk, coming toward the men's south fence gate. Edgar burped loudly, unzipped his pants, and urinated through the gate, into the yard.

Jonah patiently waited for Edgar to stumble out of sight before raising his head again. He had an idea. "If I don't eat last meal tomorrow, I'll go in the hole. If you don't eat, we'll both be outside."

Arva shook her head. "Hilda sticks me with a needle; I go right to sleep."

"Yeah," Arva's logic swept away his confidence in the plan. "Edgar does that too. Then I guess I'll…" His sentence dissolved into silence, leaving him chewing on his lip.

"Do you get a red pill?" she whispered hopefully.

Jonah nodded, starting to catch on. "If we had enough red, we wouldn't get sleepy." He scratched the filthy rat's nest that was his head with long fingernails, thinking through his next suggestion before blurting it out. "Wait and save them up?"

She shook her head. "We can't wait anymore." Her voice was powerfully cold, the words making his soul tingle. She was right; they had to escape, and they had to do it soon.

CHAPTER 15

Dr. Selleck rocked back in his chair, his feet up on the desk. The bottle of whiskey in his lap was much lighter than it had been twenty minutes ago, when he first opened it, but his mind wasn't getting any lighter. He had finally come to terms with thoughts and emotions he had been shunning for a decade—well, almost two decades in *real* time.

Edgar sat wordlessly in the cushioned inmates' chair, holding his own bottle of whiskey, his eyes shrouded behind a veil of black hair. Unlike Dr. Selleck's, Edgar's background didn't include traditional military service; he was one of the millions who had taken an opportunity to leave prison in exchange for leaving everything else too.

The Prison Militia, as they came to be known during the war of species, were more or less mercenaries that were thrown at the front lines, combat fodder that would absorb initial IIL attacks while the real military troops mobilized. Militia veterans were given amnesty for their previous offenses upon discharge, regardless of what crimes they had previously committed, and were allowed to settle in the colonies as societal equals. The probability of a Prison Militia member actually surviving until their discharge date, however, was very low, which meant that Edgar must have been very lucky, or one hell of a fighter.

Dr. Selleck never asked Edgar what he had been in for, but it must have been bad. Even with the amnesty, lifers, rapists, and murderers had a hard time integrating into the law-abiding population of the colonies after the war. Edgar had been with the camp since the very beginning, even longer than Headmaster Green, and Cydonia camp staff members were strictly volunteers. In a way, Dr. Selleck would rather not know what crimes Edgar had committed.

Ropy chunks of oily hair parted as Edgar tipped his bottle back and wiped his mouth with a fist as large as a small bowling ball. The two men never spoke much; tonight they were extra-quiet. Order number 20 and their baby had been served to the Masters yesterday, and Charlie threw himself into oblivion only hours later. Minutes ago, Headmaster Green had announced that another prisoner was about to be liquidated, possibly two.

Liquidation timelines were being sped up by the Masters, and Dr. Selleck didn't like any of the implications associated with such a drastic change in routine. Nothing new ever happened in camp unless there was a reason, and the reason was always something bad, frightening, or both.

Since the Masters wanted to eat lamb and carrots together, Arva's pending murder made sense. She was just a side dish anyway; her taste didn't matter as much, and wasn't as valuable, as Charlie's lamb-infused flesh. Charlie was dead; she should go too. That, he understood.

However, killing Jonah and Arva in the same night went against the terms of the contract. Liquidation of both meant five bodies, not including the infant, were being out-processed in less than seventy-two hours, one body over the agreed-upon limit.

The Headmaster's unexpected announcement that Arva, and maybe Jonah, would die this evening had set Dr. Selleck's consciousness off in a gloomy direction, making certain questions arise. How many Masters were down there? How hungry could they be? And even scarier: If they could so easily breach the terms of the contract, what other unexpected changes might be coming?

Product orders were arranged years in advance and meticulously tracked by the Masters, so their sudden haphazard approach to lot liquidation was setting off alarms. If they attacked, he couldn't run (no vehicles, IILs were everywhere); he couldn't fight (no weapons, no explosives, no courage); he was screwed no matter which way he looked at it.

Long ago, he learned that the Masters concocted their flavored human dishes from cookbooks, including the concept of aging and brining lamb before consuming it. Unbeknownst to Charlie, his seemingly perpetual incarceration resulted from a random turn of the page. As the camp's physician, Dr. Selleck had a duty to provide care to the prisoners. Instead, he was facilitating their execution, just so that some monster could sample an interesting recipe.

Dr. Selleck took a long drink from the bottle, hoping the stinging fluid would cleanse the guilt from his soul as it trickled into his nauseated stomach. They were waiting for the humping noises to end in Headmaster Green's office, and it sounded like activities were just now wrapping up.

Hilda liked to have her way with them once in a while, and she chose the Headmaster first tonight. The men never expressed jealousy over who was chosen first, or not chosen at all; Hilda just had a large sexual appetite. After two consecutive long days, four murders, and a money exchange with the colonies, he wasn't interested anyway. He felt dead inside.

Headmaster Green's office door suddenly opened, and relieved, drunken laughter spilled out into the hallway. The Headmaster opened Dr. Selleck's door while tucking in his shirt. A crooked smile hung below a head of disheveled, greasy hair, and his red-streaked eyes were swimming in liquor.

Edgar eagerly got to his feet and pushed his way past Headmaster Green, storming into the office across the hall. Through the door crack, just before Edgar shut the door, Dr. Selleck caught a glimpse of Hilda lying naked on the floor, covered in paper money.

Headmaster Green slicked his hair back with both hands, shut Dr. Selleck's door, and strolled to the liquor shelf, where he selected a glass and a bottle of vodka. The doctor gulped down two swallows of whiskey and wiped his mouth. Neither man was going to enjoy this.

Ostensibly reading his mind, Headmaster Green slowly pulled the guest chair over to the desk and sat down, looking Dr. Selleck squarely in the eyes. He poured a small pool of vodka into his glass, sat back, breathed out, and smiled. "What's the matter, Nick?"

Dr. Selleck stared back, adrenaline slowly eroding his alcohol buzz. "The usual."

Headmaster Green retrieved a thick envelope from his inside jacket pocket and tossed it on the desk. The doctor ignored it. "Your share of the bonus is forty thousand," Headmaster Green said, impressed with himself. "As always, I can give it to you in gold if you want. It's up to you."

Dr. Selleck tipped the bottle back and forced four large gulps down, finishing it. He opened his desk drawer, retrieved a fresh bottle of whiskey, and unscrewed the top.

The Headmaster's face fell. "They're unwanted fetuses, donated products. Get over it."

"Long time ago, that's exactly what they were to me, just assholes in the way," Dr. Selleck said, a little surprised at how crisp his voice was after he'd downed a fifth of Jack Daniel's in thirty minutes. "Money was the only thing that mattered to me then."

Headmaster Green laughed and took another sip from his glass. "Nothing wrong with being a rich pioneer."

"But when you have to know them, treat them through childbirth, lot after lot, just so my envelope is extra-tight..." He took his legs off the desk, leaned forward, and picked up the envelope. He squeezed it and then let it fall.

"It's been too many." Doctor Selleck watched the Headmaster launch into his routine of pretending to understand and agree with him. First the fake grin, then the soft eyes and a slow nod.

"Could be worse," Headmaster Green said sensibly, "like it was before the contracts and the Cydonia camps, when this was all a GCMC base, not a kindergarten for whore abortions and abandoned infants.

"Remember those days? Night attacks, entire settlements slaughtered; destruction and war across the entire planet. They took down a hundred years of progress and killed fifty thousand colonists in a month."

It sounded logical from the outside looking in, but Dr. Selleck knew better. It was a murder camp, not a kindergarten. "I've only seen the Masters once, in that little cubbyhole below your office, where you kiss their scaly asses," he said condescendingly. "Recently, I've been seeing Giants in the forest beyond the main gate; big, mean-looking bastards that could rip down the fence in a few seconds.

"Obviously, I never see the Giants at night, because I keep my shutters closed like a good little boy. It was during the day, when they're not supposed to be out." He gleefully watched all pretense vanish from the Headmaster's face. He was really getting under Headmaster Green's skin and enjoying every second of it.

"If they're getting active in the day, what are we going to do?" Dr. Selleck asked sarcastically and took a swig from the freshly opened whiskey bottle.

Annoyed and practicing restraint, Headmaster Green gathered his thoughts. The next phase would be the big payoff, lot liquidation, and he couldn't afford problems with the staff. "Do you know Headmaster Krupps?"

Dr. Selleck nodded; his memory was still functioning, but he couldn't picture the guy. "You were in prison together back home."

"He had Cydonia 11, big camp, sixteen inmates, about two miles from the pyramids."

"Had?" Dr. Selleck asked flatly, knowing he had fallen into a conversation trap.

"Governor said it's been overrun, everyone killed, inmates and staff."

The words sank in slowly. Dr. Selleck suddenly found himself feeling helpless. "When did this happen?"

"About three weeks ago," the Headmaster said flippantly as he refilled his glass with vodka. "Product broke out of his cell at night and—get this—tried to touch one of the Giants through the fence, pet it like it was a dog or something. Now there's only eleven camps."

"Because he tried to touch it?" Dr. Selleck didn't want to believe the story, but he knew deep down that it was true.

"Because the inmate gave it reason to attack. He violated the terms of the contract by being outside at night; it's that simple. The Masters and the Giants don't share the products, they *compete* for them. The Giant was looking for a reason to take out the entire camp, and it got one. Now we owe the Masters an entire new lot, and they get it for free."

"Speaking of contracts, wouldn't Jonah push us over the threshold? Five in seventy-two hours is one over." At this point, Dr. Selleck couldn't discern if he was actually making sense or if he was babbling. Too many numbers had just come out of his mouth at once.

The Headmaster did his best to pretend to be concerned. "It's their inventory, Nick. If they want the entire lot tonight, I'll give it to them. But they would have to pay bonuses for every single one of them, and I don't think they have the money for that, do you?"

"If they're breaking terms, what if they decide to come up here and kill us all?"

"Then we die." The silence that followed was suddenly broken as the Headmaster added vodka to his glass and sealed the bottle.

Dr. Selleck leaned back in his chair and put his feet up on the desk again, partly stabilizing himself, but also to pull back from the conversation. Sometimes he forgot where he was and the situation he had put himself into. Why hadn't he gone back home when he had the chance?

"Sometimes, in the meetings with the Masters, when I'm kissing their scaly asses in the little cubbyhole below my office, I see it in their eyes." The Headmaster's mocking tone bounced off its target.

"Death," Dr. Selleck said quietly, echoing the thoughts ricocheting through his mind.

"Hunger," Headmaster Green slowly corrected, his eyes twinkling in the dim light.

* * *

5:46 P.M.

Outside, in the slowly darkening yard, Jonah contemplated a problem. He rubbed his lips, trying as hard as possible to force a brilliant idea to the forefront of his mind. He didn't want to look like an idiot in front of Arva. "We'll climb over the fence," he realized the idea was going nowhere as the words dribbled from his mouth, "and then find a place to live in the woods," he finished, disappointed.

"The fence is too high," Arva said, annoyed. "Plus the animals in the woods would kill us. I saw one during exercise once, and they're really scary-looking!"

"I'll throw you over the fence, then we'll…" This time, he couldn't bring himself to conclude the sentence.

"Jonah, female 19 escaped—we have to try it that way, like we already talked about."

"You don't think the fence is better?"

Frustrated, Arva calmed herself, knowing that they had to outline a plan here and now if it was going to be successful. They couldn't keep in contact through notes in the yard. "Know what to do tomorrow?" she asked hopefully.

Jonah reluctantly nodded. "Don't eat last meal."

"Before that," she snapped, momentarily losing control of the volume of her voice. Except for sleeping inmates, the yard was empty.

"I really want to ask him, just once. If he says no, I'll just take a handful and put it in my pants."

"If you ask him, he'll tell. We can't risk it, OK?"

Arva's bright green eyes were mesmerizing. Right now, she could tell Jonah anything and he would go along. Escaping together meant being able to touch her, and he had longed for that as far back as his memory of her could go.

"Take them, don't ask," she said sharply.

* * *

5:49 P.M.

Headmaster Green emptied the bottle into his glass, his shaky pouring technique letting ten percent of the liquor splatter across the desk. "Oops," he said shamelessly, and wiped it off with his hand.

Dr. Selleck was too numb to care. "So, we're taking Arva out tonight, right?"

"She knew something was wrong with the food and wine. We're already bleeding profit because of the fucking idiot last night. Fuck it," Headmaster Green slurred. "Not looking forward to stripping a girl naked tonight, not after what Hilda just did to me at least. God, the inmates really stink sometimes, don't they?"

"Especially in the summertime." Dr. Selleck sipped on his

bottle, unable to drink much more. His stomach was sending signals that he would soon be vomiting; might as well save the rest for the next drinking binge. "How about Jonah?" He nervously awaited a response, his belly cramping.

The Headmaster smiled, studying him. "Male 24? They said no, and we'll wait. They still have confidence in our ability to prevent him from escaping, even with what happened. Male 25—" Headmaster Green ironically laughed "—really screwed us. Including the girl, penalty is over a million. A million!" he proclaimed loudly, as if the doctor hadn't heard him the first time.

Relieved at the news, the tightness in Dr. Selleck's intestines loosened. "How much was the aging bonus on him? I'm just curious."

Even in his vodka fog, Headmaster Green could smell passive-aggressive rebellion all over the good doctor. "Eight hundred thousand; imagine splitting that five ways. Make it even worse, the Governor wants a bigger cut. He's got one less camp to spread out costs, a new facility needs to be built, and new products need to be drawn from the transition camp. All of these problems mean that order 22 has to work out extra-perfect."

Dr. Selleck smiled, eating up the fake concern being fed to him. "What do you need?"

Headmaster Green shrugged, attempting to convince him that the idea hadn't been rehearsed in private. "Increase their dosage, by a lot."

"Just jack them up with fertility pills and see what happens." Dr. Selleck nodded his head, acting like he agreed with the idea. "They could get cancer, but then again who gives a shit?" He took another sip, fighting the urge to throw the bottle at the Headmaster.

"Triplets or better, we're back on track for fiscal-year goals, including bonuses. We give the Governor his inflated cut, we keep whatever's left."

Dr. Selleck laughed, his bellyful of whiskey jostling uncomfortably in the process. Although the Headmaster was a scumbag, he knew about numbers. "After Jonah and Edith, when the lot is liquidated, I'm getting a ticket back."

The Headmaster's surprise was genuine. "Yesterday, we talked about an extension, worked through the timeline and everything. Now you want out?"

"Changed my mind; I should have got out after the last lot, but I didn't. That's my mistake."

Headmaster Green shifted forward, anger bubbling in his alcohol-soaked insides. "New units were purchased based on our conversation. They arrive two days after we clean house. The Masters want to see supplement schedules next week!"

"I'll give you a dosage charge, you bullshit your way through it," Dr. Selleck replied blandly. "You're a great bullshitter." He let the Headmaster stew as he pulled another short drink from the bottle. "So, the new lot, anything unusual?"

Headmaster Green slowly nodded, his thoughts turning dark. "Female 28—they want her to taste like herbs, haven't decided which ones yet." He got up from the chair and slowly stumbled toward the window, where he looked out into the yard and then up to the sky. "It's late; the products need to be stored."

He turned from the window, patted Dr. Selleck on the back, and walked to the door, opening it. He turned back, giving it one last shot. "You could always take a vacation instead of quitting on me. And the fee will increase for the next lot, by five percent. Think about it—maybe you'll change your mind again."

"If you try to stop me, I'll ruin everything for you. Then there'll only be ten camps."

The Headmaster gritted his teeth, nodded to acknowledge understanding, and exited the office, slamming the door behind him.

CHAPTER 16

Jonah stood with Barry at the Lines of Division, looking across the yard at the front wall of the women's barracks, where he found the shuttered window of female 25, the green-eyed beauty named Arva. The two never quite worked out a perfect plan the previous evening, as Edgar, Hilda, and Headmaster Green interrupted their conversation by stumbling into the yard from the administration area.

The three staff members had quickly hoisted sleeping bodies from the ground and dumped them back in their cells. Jonah shut his eyes the moment he saw Headmaster Green walking crookedly across the yard toward him and only opened them when the lock of his cell had clicked into place.

He didn't know what had happened to Arva, and he feared the worst, but decided to assume that she had been taken back to her cell too. This morning, however, her shutters weren't open. Female 23, Barry's opposite number, was not at her un-shuttered window, but the long-faced, ugly girl that was Jonah's opposite number was in her usual place—longingly staring out her window at him.

Jonah now had a better understanding of why Mitch had acted the way he did. After his marriage, Mitch seemed to care only about female 20 and the time he had shared with her. Arva was the only thing Jonah could think about now, and not seeing her was driving him crazy.

"It feels weird, just you and me out here," Barry mused as he looked out over the abandoned yard.

"Where is she?" Jonah demanded, ignoring him.

Barry's brow wrinkled; he followed Jonah's angry glare to the shutters closed over female 25's window and realized what was wrong, "Must have left last night. Maybe Charlie came back for her or something."

Jonah's head slowly turned, his teeth barely containing an explosion of anger. "He didn't come back, Barry, don't you remember? I told you what happened!"

"Yeah, I was thinking, you might have dreamed it, Jonah, like I dream about Edgar chasing me and beating me with a beef tongue. It's not real, but it's still scary. I have dreams like that all the time."

Jonah fumed; he could tell that Barry had been working on the explanation, and the thought of him sitting in his cell, thinking through the idiocy of it all, annoyed Jonah to no end. "I felt the monster next to me; it drooled on me! There was sticky water stuff all over the floor the next day, and the excretion duct is still broken!" he was shouting, and didn't care who heard him.

Barry tightened his burlap blanket around himself, hurt by Jonah's tone. "Look, I'm right after Richard. I'm next! Less than a year and I'm out."

"I don't give a shit about what you think happened in your cell *when you were dreaming*," Barry emphasized, "and I don't care about what happened last night. I…" Something miraculous overtook Barry's face. He was having a thought. "What happened last night, anyway?" he asked innocently.

Jonah massaged frustration from the bridge of his nose. "If I escape, will you go?"

Barry's countenance shifted to smug defiance. "Less than a year and I'm out."

Edgar appeared at the south gate and opened it, drawing their attention. The large man was walking slowly and seemed grumpy. They would have to tread lightly today.

Edgar stopped just inside the yard. "Twenty-four!" he yelled, wincing from the pain shooting through his skull. "Doctor's appointment!" Jonah shuffled away, leaving Barry alone at the Lines of Division.

* * *

8:19 A.M.

Edith sighed, watching her future marriage partner slink off through the men's-side south gate and disappear into the administration area. Bored, and not caring about male 23's activities, she wandered to the wall that she shared with Beth and peered through the knothole into the adjacent cell. Beth sat against the opposing wall in a daze. Normally, she would be watching men's exercise instead of blankly staring off into space.

"You look like shit," Edith said with a smirk. Beth appeared to have been up all night. Her eyes were dark and swollen, and her dirty blond hair was clumpier than usual. When Edith received no reply, she tried a different tone. "I guess Arva left," she said meekly.

Beth ignored her. After a pregnant silence, Edith tried again. "She must have—"

"What did you say to the Headmaster?" Beth barked at her accusingly. Sharp eyes shot death through the knothole, making Edith pull back from it.

Edith mentally scanned through the many things she had told Headmaster Green, and decided to confess to none. "What? I didn't say anything."

"You talked to him at the food table, and Hilda; I watched you!"

Tears welled in Edith's eyes; all of her pain and frustration poured out with them. "Arva kept looking at him! What about me, Beth? Who do I get to look at?" Initially a whimper, Edith's side of the story ended in a scream.

Beth got up and walked to the wall and stared through the knothole, not hearing anything Edith was saying. "She's dead because of you."

"She left camp; she was supposed to go!"

"Something took her through her excretion duct, dragged her down into the basement. Just like Carol. And it was all because of you, just because you didn't like her looking at him." Beth's memory of it was too vivid, the details horrifyingly quick to retrieve from her memory. The event flooded back the instant she began to talk about it.

* * *

SEPTEMBER 14, 2335 M.E.
10:31 P.M.

It was after the feast, and well after sundown. The vibration of a loud thump coming from Arva's cell woke her up, but it was the talking that made her stay awake. Although Beth's head was spinning and her mind slow-moving, she recognized Headmaster Green's voice. The Headmaster never came to the women's barracks at nighttime, and neither did anyone else.

A bright beam of light poured into Beth's cell through the knothole that she and Arva used for conversation. The light was too bright to be Arva's cell bulb; something unusual was afoot, and Beth loved mysteries. She carefully got out of bed and walked to the wall, making sure to avoid squeaky floorboards as she tiptoed up to the knothole.

The light was coming from a bright lantern that was sitting on Arva's feeding table. Beth's eye darted from Headmaster Green to Hilda, who were both standing over Arva's unmoving body. Hilda held a long needle, the same one she used on prisoners just before putting them in the hole, but the inmates were never taken to the hole after sundown.

As he looked down at Arva, Headmaster Green ran his hand nervously over his greasy hair and checked his watch. "Strip off the uniform and leave her by the duct," he grumbled.

Hilda kneeled down and produced a knife, but she paused before cutting through the burlap. "I thought they eat the head first. Shouldn't we shave—?"

"Strip it off, don't cut it off!" Headmaster Green snapped, interrupting her, and pointed to Arva's collar. Hilda sheathed the knife and began tugging on Arva's uniform top.

"We need the material for the next lot, and we have to hurry," he said sarcastically. "And to answer your question, we don't have time to shave her head—it's already nighttime!" The veins in Headmaster Green's head were about to burst.

"I don't trust them, even when they're feeding, and I don't want to become dessert just because I'm walking back to my bunk at night. Do you?"

Hilda didn't even look up to answer him; she just continued removing Arva's uniform.

Headmaster Green checked his watch again and breathed out, frustrated by the pace of progress. He knelt next to Arva's feet and began tugging on the cuffs of her uniform bottoms.

After Arva was naked, Headmaster Green and Hilda quickly exited the cell with Arva's uniform, blanket, and feeding plate. Hilda remembered the lantern but forgot to click off the cell bulb, letting the next events unfold without any visual hindrance.

"Arva," Beth hissed in a loud whisper, but Arva didn't move. "Arva!" she said desperately, hoping the Headmaster and Hilda hadn't heard her. A beating usually resulted from breaking the rule of silence, but the risk was worth taking. Why would Hilda stick Arva with a needle and leave her alone in her cell?

Beth waited patiently by the knothole for over an hour, fighting the urge to sleep. Noises echoing in the basement suddenly dismissed any trace of tiredness; the amorphous thumps and scrapes coming from below were getting louder by the second, and then abruptly stopped.

She clung to consciousness as she stood at the wall. Her body wanted to go back to bed so badly, but her eyes wouldn't let her leave the knothole. A loud bang from under Arva's excretion duct hatch jolted Beth with adrenaline, making her jump, and took the hatch off its hinges.

The last thing Beth remembered was a long, clawed hand curling around the top of the duct, and unbridled fear erupting through her soul. The combination made her dizzy. The hand was brownish-gray and scaly, the claws were dirty and sharp, and it was coming for her best friend, who lay motionless less than a foot away from the duct.

She wanted to scream out, but fear paralyzed her; then everything went dark.

She woke up on the floor the next day. The moment consciousness hit her, she jumped to her feet and looked through the knothole, frantically searching for Arva. The broken hatch still lay where it had landed the previous night, and a murky white liquid discolored the floor around the duct.

* * *

SEPTEMBER 15, 2335 M.E.
8:34 A.M.

Beth blinked; inside, she was happy seeing the look of shock and horror on Edith's face, but they were past that now. Edith wasn't an enemy to pick on anymore, she was dead to her. "I'm never talking to you again," Beth announced in a calm, clear voice. She walked away from the knothole, turned her back to the wall and leaned on it, then slowly slid to the ground.

Her mind slipped back into yet another replay of the previous evening, and her eyes glazed over. If she could have seen into the room next to hers, she would have found Edith wedged into the corner of her cell, wrapped into a human ball and sobbing.

CHAPTER 17

As Dr. Selleck cut Jonah's filthy fingernails, Jonah's nervous eyes drifted to the open cabinet full of pills to his right. Bucket-sized containers full of various colored pills, including red pills, were stacked within reaching distance. His plan was simple: if Dr. Selleck gave him the opportunity, he would take a handful of red and shove them in his pants. Meanwhile, Jonah couldn't remember the last time he was alone in the office, so he might have to do it when the doctor turned his back.

Dr. Selleck finished Jonah's right hand, collected the discarded fingernail clippings, and threw them in the trashcan. He picked up Jonah's left hand and felt it tremble. "Something you want to talk about?" he asked casually.

Jonah's eyes widened. "No, I..." He thought about it for a moment. "No," he squeaked out, and forced a fake smile.

Dr. Selleck smirked and began trimming Jonah's fingernails again. "Your heart rate was way up when I checked you, your hand is shaking, and you're not talking. That combination tells me you're nervous about something," he said as he clipped away shards of Jonah's fingernail.

Jonah gulped. Arva had disagreed with him asking Dr. Selleck for help; then again, he probably wouldn't have a chance to take the pills without being seen. He decided to take a leap of faith. "Did female 19 escape?" he asked, doing his best to make the question sound calm.

Dr. Selleck finished Jonah's smallest finger, tossed the nail clippings into the trash, and sat down on a small stool outfitted with rusty wheels. "Now who did you hear that from?" he queried carefully.

"Mitch and Charlie," he blurted.

"She actually did escape, a long time ago." They stared at each other for a moment, a thin wall of pretense wobbling between them.

"Through the fence?" Jonah prodded warily.

"No." Dr. Selleck closed the cabinet and locked it, then pocketed the key. "Inmates can't escape that way, because of sensor implants." Jonah's eyes squinted and his brow furrowed. "Sensor implants are small machines in your body that come alive when you touch the fence or even get near it. These machines tell everyone who's watching you where you are and what you're doing."

Jonah nodded, understanding. "The guards would know right away once I touch the fence." Dr. Selleck ignored him and reached for a steel tray lined with syringes of varying sizes and colors. Jonah, used to being stuck with needles, lay back in the chair and relaxed. "Female 19 got out though," he said thoughtfully.

"OK, sleeve up," Dr. Selleck ordered, and Jonah raised his uniform sleeve up to the shoulder. Jonah eyed the tray, recognizing the mix of colors. Dr. Selleck followed Jonah's gaze to the orange syringe. "You have a question about the needles?"

"The orange one makes me really sleepy. Even if I want to say awake, I can't."

Dr. Selleck nodded. "The one Edgar uses—this one—though, is an eighth dose, a smaller dose," he added.

"It's kind of like orange pills, but a lot of them at once," Jonah awkwardly surmised.

Dr. Selleck was impressed. "That's good; orange pills are made of the same thing. The more you get, the sleepier you get."

"What about red pills?" Jonah inadvertently glanced at the cabinet and the jug of red pills inside it.

Dr. Selleck smiled. "Red pills make you alert, happy, and awake. They're also called amphetamines." He took the plastic tip off of the first syringe and injected Jonah with a green solution.

"That's a big word," Jonah said, unable to remember the word, much less pronounce it. "I get one red, and three orange, along with other stuff."

"I know; I fill your prescription."

"If I took a lot of red at once, what would happen?" Jonah asked, blatantly revealing the purpose of the question.

"It depends—if you took, say, five red pills, you wouldn't get sleepy, even if Edgar injected you with the orange needle. So remember, five." Dr. Selleck raised his hand and pointed to his fingers as he counted, "One, two, three, four, and five. If you take any more than that at once, you could die."

The bluntness of the statement was lost on Jonah, who just greedily nodded. "Charlie said he used to get yellow pills, a long time ago, back when he got married the first time."

Dr. Selleck raised his eyebrows, surprised at how much Jonah and the other prisoners analyzed pills. "That's true. Richard and female 22 get yellow pills now. A lot of them," he said ironically, more to himself than Jonah.

Dr. Selleck moved on to the blue needles as Jonah shifted uncomfortably in the chair.

"Have you ever seen the guards?" Jonah asked suddenly.

Dr. Selleck almost forgot what he was doing. His steely gaze met Jonah's eyes. "Yes, I have," he said slowly. He resumed the injections, forcing himself not to lose track of the dosages, his mind running back through the depressing internal maze it had been lost in since the previous evening.

"I haven't, ever. Sometimes I think they're not real." Jonah studied the doctor's face for any sign of malice.

"You don't want to meet them, trust me."

"I wonder… how did female 19 get past them?" Jonah's attempt at nonchalance fell miserably short.

Dr. Selleck finished the last injection, a low dose of the opioids all inmates became hooked on by the end of their first week in camp, and sat back, hanging his head as he deliberated over what to say next. The last few days had changed him, including his outlook on the prisoners. Jonah was smart and determined; the world would be a better place with him in it.

"The guards have a feast the same time we do, but they fall asleep for a long time afterward, sometimes for days. I'm thinking, and this is just a guess, she was very quiet and somehow sneaked around them while they were sleeping.

"Her sensor implants—the things we were just talking about— were scanned somewhere across the border, so she definitely escaped. What happened after that?" he asked rhetorically and shrugged. "Who knows?"

Jonah's mind raced through the overabundance of information, fixating only on a few key elements. "The guards are probably asleep today then, and tonight."

"They can wake up, so be careful." Dr. Selleck winked at him and then turned to his desk, where he started marking up paperwork with a pen.

Unsure of what to do next, Jonah slowly got up from the chair and walked out of the office, stealing one last look at the locked cabinet of pills before he closed the door. Tears welled in Dr. Selleck's eyes as the door shut. He pushed away the papers he had been pretending to write on, dropped his head into his hands, and quietly sobbed.

If he did this thing, there was no going back. But it was the right thing to do, and it gave him a chance at redemption. He wiped away tears and sniffled, then slowly resumed writing out weekly reports. Each pen stroke felt important, as if he were writing a suicide note.

CHAPTER 18

As Edgar served him his last feeding, Jonah skipped his usual examination and evaluation of the broccoli. His mind was too focused on the invisible contents of the numbered pill bag that lay somewhere within Edgar's apron pocket to care about complaining. "Pills, please," Jonah said nervously.

Annoyed, Edgar breathed out and scooped more broccoli sprouts onto Jonah's dented plate. "Yeah, yeah, hold on." The large man put the metal pot back onto the cart in the hallway and dug into his pocket. He retrieved two bags, isolated the one marked 24, and tossed it onto Jonah's feeding table.

Jonah recognized a large glut of red in the bag before it even landed.

Edgar exited the cell and locked it. Sounds of the cart moving, and the click of Barry's cell being opened, told Jonah that he could act relatively freely. He pushed his plate of broccoli back and dumped the bag of pills onto his feeding table. He lined them up and touched each red with a different finger as he counted. "One, four, three, four, five," he said. Although he failed to mimic Dr.

Selleck's precision, he had correctly adhered to the process. The doctor had done his part; now all Jonah had to do was get outside.

He gathered the three orange pills and walked over to his excretion duct. He kicked off the broken hatch that was uneasily sitting on top of the duct and stood over the stinking hole, holding his precious allotment of orange pills. He had to fulfill his promise to Arva, regardless of how much his body was telling his mind to eat the opioid pills and give in to addiction.

The pills dropped into the darkness below, dragging regret down with them. He put the hatch back on its crooked perch, retrieved the red and blue pills from the feeding table, and washed them down with water. Nervous and shaking, he set the cup on his feeding table, walked to his door, and looked through the notch.

Edgar closed Barry's cell door, clicked the lock shut, and turned toward the food cart. "Edgar!" Jonah shouted, making Edgar jump from surprise. "I'm not eating."

"What?" he demanded with a snarl.

"I'm tired of eating broccoli. I don't want to do it anymore." Jonah meant it. He was about to risk his life to ensure that he never ate broccoli again. As Edgar trudged toward his cell, he backed up and sat down on his chair, knowing too well the brutal force that was about to explode at him.

Edgar threw the door open and kicked Jonah in the chest, knocking the wind out of him, toppling the chair over backward, and slamming his head hard against the floor. The hulking enforcer stood over him, a look of madness in his eyes.

"Pick up your plate!" he growled. Jonah scurried to his feet and reclaimed his broccoli, as his lungs fought to take in oxygen. Edgar shoved him out into the hallway and closed the cell door.

Jonah coughed and staggered as he slowly regained the ability to breathe, balancing his plate precariously as he gasped for air. He leaned against Barry's door with his free hand, his chest heaving; he looked up and found his friend's eyes staring back at him through the door notch.

Barry slowly nodded. "I'll go," he whispered meekly, as Edgar secured the lock on Jonah's cell. Jonah nodded back, burning the memory of the moment into his mind, just in case it was the last time he saw Barry. Jonah was about to risk his life, and they both knew it.

"Shut up in there, 23, or you'll lose some teeth when I'm through with him." Edgar gathered the flashlight and the baton from the food cart, then rudely pushed Jonah down the hallway, to the barracks door.

Jonah stepped over the threshold, into the yard, and suddenly tripped, nearly scattering the broccoli all over the grass. "You drop any, you eat it off the ground," Edgar said through gritted teeth. He wrapped a chain around the door's steel handles and closed the lock. He was pushing it on time, but he didn't want to hear the Headmaster's bitching about not following protocol. When an inmate refused his plate, he had to go in the hole.

The yard was dimly lit, with the sun low on the horizon, and the pre-fall air was crisp and cool. Jonah was past the hard part: getting out of his cell before nighttime, with enough red pills in his system to keep him awake. The rest of the plan, however, was a bit blurry.

As they marched toward the south fence, Edgar jabbed him in the back with the butt of the flashlight, urging his pace to increase. Edgar was worried about something and kept looking at the top of the trees, where the sun was setting.

Jonah eyed the distant isolation hole on the female side of the Lines of Division, his heart thumping in his chest; it was exposed and appeared empty. Arva was supposed to be out there with him— they were supposed to be escaping together. Maybe she was still in her cell; maybe she didn't want to wait for him and got out already; maybe the monsters took her. Racing thoughts ricocheted through his skull, each more terrible than the last.

The hair rose up on the back of his neck as he imagined wandering alone in the forest, or wherever he ended up after he got out, and not having pills, water, or food. He gulped, suddenly frightened by the reality of what he was about to do.

As the hole loomed closer, he forced his mind to refocus on the second phase of the escape and forget everything else. He could worry about surviving without pills after he got out. Plus, Arva still had time to refuse her plate and get thrown into the hole too; he couldn't give up on her yet.

Ten feet from the crudely fashioned ditch, Edgar swiped the back of Jonah's left leg out with the flashlight, making him fall. He dropped to his knees, miraculously managing not to drop his plate.

"Stay down there," Edgar ordered, "eat it like a dog." Jonah didn't know what a dog was, but he did as instructed and stayed on his hands and knees. "With no hands!" Edgar said menacingly. Jonah complied, using his chin and upper teeth to corral the broccoli and pick it up.

A few bites later, Edgar clicked on the flashlight, checking to see what was left. "Hurry up, 24!" he spat, and surveyed the fence line. "And each smudge I find, I'm breaking a rib."

Jonah licked the plate clean as he chewed on the last sprig of broccoli. Edgar scanned the plate with his flashlight, grunted in disapproval, and kneed Jonah in the chest. Half-chewed broccoli spilled out over Jonah's neck and uniform.

"Put it back in your mouth!" Edgar shouted.

A steady flood of energy was increasing in pressure inside Jonah's chest, and it wasn't just a bruise the size of Edgar's boot that was causing the sensation. The red pills were working, more than he had expected. He scooped up the broccoli and consumed it, as Edgar dragged the heavy stone off of the wooden plank lying nearby.

With labored breathing, Edgar yanked Jonah to his feet, rolled up his sleeve, and jabbed him roughly in the forearm with a large needle full of orange liquid. When he was finished, he shoved Jonah into the grave-sized hole and dragged the wooden plank over it. Before letting the plank fall, Edgar offered a parting gift.

"Nighty-night," he said psychotically and spat on Jonah's face. Edgar dropped the plank and rolled the stone back on top of it, dusting his hands off afterward. As he speed-walked through the south gate, he closed the latch but purposely left the chain dangling and the lock open. Nighttime was upon them; there was no time to waste.

On the way to his bunk, Edgar nervously checked every corner of the administration area with a flashlight. He cursed himself for not taking his gun with him during the last feeding.

* * *

7:13 P.M.

Jonah sat in the silence and darkness of the hole for a few minutes before moving, wondering the entire time if the floating feeling in his head meant that the effects of the orange needle were too much for the red pills to overcome. But he was still awake and feeling good.

Just like Edgar, Hilda only brought female inmates to the isolation hole before the sun went down. It was nighttime; there was no reason to keep waiting. He tried pushing on the center of the wooden plank that covered the hole, hoping to lift it up all at once, but the stone on top was too heavy, and he had no leverage whatsoever. Next, he tried lifting the corner of the board, at the end of the ditch, just above his head. His already-high heart rate increased even more when the board successfully came away from the ground.

Inch by inch, the plank slid over the grass, the stone wobbling slightly with each nudge. It took thirty minutes of jostling and a lot of sweat, but he eventually created enough space to wiggle out. As Jonah stood up, alone in the yard at night, feelings of isolation and abandonment swept over him. His gaze shifted to the women's barracks and to Arva's closed shutters, as panic fluttered in his chest. The opportunity to escape was at hand, but he was too afraid to do it without her. She had given him the courage to take on such a terrifyingly new experience without looking back. Without her, he felt lost.

To get into the female barracks and break Arva out, he needed Hilda's keys. To get the keys, he had to access the administration building and search room by room, while somehow avoiding the four staff members. It sounded impossible, but he had already gone this far. Crawling back in the hole and returning to a life of eating broccoli was no longer an option. He walked quickly across the chilly grass toward the south fence gate, a surreal sense of disbelief growing inside him. After all these years, was he risking everything in one random night?

An unbolted lock swayed from a chain wrapped loosely around the gate. For once, luck was on Jonah's side. He swung the creaking steel gate open, closed it behind him, and crept blindly through the darkened administration area.

Bare feet padded cautiously along the freezing concrete sidewalk that led to the administration building, a long edifice that stretched horizontally across the entire length of the southern exterior fence. Each step was taken with care; he knew that if he were caught outside like this at night, they would probably kill him.

As the administration building's row of narrow windows eventually came into view, Jonah froze. Shadows of movement flickered in the light filtering through closed shutters of the second window, which was Dr. Selleck's office. All Jonah could determine from the movement was that at least two people were in the office.

He crouched down, hurried to the north side of the building, and leaned on one hand against the wall. He cocked his ear toward the shutters, hearing muted conversation. Two people inside the doctor's office were talking to each other, and they didn't sound happy. Jonah slowly raised his eye to a small crack in the shutters and peered through.

Suddenly, loud sounds of a struggle erupted from inside the office, making Jonah cringe. Grunts, noises of exertion and strain, and a loud crash were followed by a solid thud that landed just on the other side of the shuttered window. After a good period of silence, Jonah peered through the shutters again and couldn't believe what he saw.

Edgar was on the floor, face-down in a pool of blood that was spreading with each passing second. A bloody hammer lay near his head, which was caved in. Pulpy chunks, blood, and hair were clumped together around the wound. Jonah shivered; the macabre image, the climate, and most importantly the drugs were becoming too much for his system to handle simultaneously. Being cold was nothing new, but the large dose of orange and red drugs made his limbs rubbery and his head feel oddly ethereal.

He stared at Edgar's shattered skull while chewing his lip. Edgar might have keys to the female barracks too, possibly even the cell doors. In any case, if he could retrieve Edgar's keys, he could get Barry out. Stealing keys from a dead man, however, would be no easy task. Three other staff members were still somewhere inside the building.

He skulked along the wall of shuttered windows until he was standing by the front door of the administration building. With a trembling hand, he silently opened the door and stepped inside, where warm air and a smooth floor greeted his shaking body and callused feet.

The hallway that extended the length of the building was faintly lit by three overhanging lamps and was eerily quiet. He breathed in deeply, waiting for his mind to refocus and muscle spasms to subside before moving again. Heated air eventually calmed the uncontrollable tremors in his arms and legs, but his thoughts were still crammed with noisy chaos.

Only one of the nine doors in the hallway was open—Dr. Selleck's office. The two doors closest to Jonah led into storage rooms; the doctor's office and Headmaster's office were next, followed by four small rooms, each serving as a bunk for the staff members. At the end of the hall was the darkened classroom.

Bright, moving lights were bleeding out from under the door to Hilda's bunk, the last room on the left, at the far end of the hallway. Jonah could hear unintelligible voices and sounds coming from the room, indicating that Hilda was talking with someone. He needed to get out of the hallway as quickly and as silently as possible, before they opened the door and found him.

He tiptoed toward Dr. Selleck's office, anxiety tightening in his chest with each stealthy stride. A sudden, loud thud erupted from the office, making Jonah freeze. His eyes darted back and forth between the doctor's doorway and Hilda's bunk, as awful sounds of strained breathing and pain gradually faded into silence.

Jonah hugged the hallway wall as he inched toward the open doorway, worried over who or what had made the sounds. Maybe Edgar was not dead after all; if Jonah had to fight, at least the larger man was already wounded. He stopped a foot from the doctor's office and carefully peered around the corner, using one eye to look inside.

Dr. Selleck was on the floor, leaning against the cabinet of pills, his eyes vacantly still. A thin rubber hose was wrapped around his arm, and two empty needles were on the floor next to his hand. One empty needle stuck out from his arm, the injection unfinished before his death; fresh vomit oozed from the doctor's gaping mouth. Thankfully, Edgar was still in the same place, face-down on the ground, and dead.

Jonah shuffled inside the office and squatted down next to Dr. Selleck, his mind not yet fully embracing the idea that the doctor was no longer alive. He reached out and poked the doctor's face with his index finger and got no reaction. Wanting to make sure, he tried again, this time sticking his finger in the doctor's eyeball. Dr. Selleck didn't even blink.

Grief swept through Jonah, clearing out fear, anxiety, and everything else. Dr. Selleck was a kind soul and the closest thing any of the inmates had to a father figure. And now he was gone. Jonah didn't even get a chance to say goodbye.

Tears welled up in Jonah's eyes as his right hand dove into the doctor's coat pocket and retrieved a ring of three keys. He had seen Dr. Selleck work the lock on the pill cabinet plenty of times, so he knew exactly which key to use and how to use it. The cabinet's glass doors swung open in seconds, revealing a gold mine of powerful drugs.

He grabbed a roll of plastic bags, tore off the first one, and then popped the top off of the red pill bucket. Two handfuls of red pills seemed excessive, but he filled the bag with what he selected anyway. Two handfuls of orange pills were dumped on top of the red, and then small samples of blue and brown followed.

The sound of the front door to the administration building slamming shut made fear shoot through Jonah's spine. He dashed to the office door and slowly closed it, quietly turning the knob while pushing the door flush with the wall as footsteps in the hallway clicked toward him.

He crouched down, leaned against the wall, and stared at the knob with wide eyes, hoping it remained still. Just below the knob was what appeared to be a metal key, but it was attached directly to the door. As the footsteps got louder, he reached out and turned the key to the right, and heard a lock click into place. Jonah tugged on the key, unable to pry it loose no matter how hard he tried.

Sweat dripped down the back of his neck and pooled in his armpits as the feet stomping down the hallway came to a stop in front of Dr. Selleck's office. The mysterious person suddenly knocked on the door three times, sending loud reverberations through the surrounding wall and making Jonah almost jump out of his skin.

With both Dr. Selleck and Edgar dead, and Hilda in her bunk, the person at the door could be only one man, and he was the most dangerous and cruel of them all.

The knob began to turn; Jonah held his breath, but the door didn't open. Headmaster Green's invisible feet abruptly turned away and walked down the hallway. Jonah released a lungful of air, slowly recovering from the wave of anxiety. He heard a distant knock and pressed his ear to the office door.

"Sorry to interrupt, but have you seen Nick or Edgar?" he heard Headmaster Green ask.

"I think they're at the still; Doctor was supposed to fix it," Hilda replied, seemingly annoyed. "It was leaking or something."

"It's well after seven, though, so that doesn't add up."

A long silence was eventually broken by Hilda's voice. "I don't know where they are; I haven't seen them."

Headmaster Green ignored her icy, forceful tone. "There's a problem with the pill count. Your numbers check out; Edgar's don't. If you see Edgar or Nick, tell them to come see me so we can figure out what happened."

"OK, I will."

Jonah heard Hilda's door shut and Headmaster Green walking toward him once again. The Headmaster turned into his office, directly across the hall from Dr. Selleck's office, and swung the door partially closed. Somewhere in Hilda's room, a bizarre sound came to life. Jonah had never heard music before; the thudding drums, buzzing guitars, and wailing vocals were completely foreign to his ears. Although they were obnoxiously loud and horribly unpleasant to listen to, the strange noises would make it easier for him to operate unnoticed.

Jonah contemplated his next set of actions as he gathered energy. Only two staff members were left, and both were formidable adversaries. Taking them on together or even one on one would be suicide. Avoiding them altogether was ideal but unrealistic. He also couldn't stay where he was; eventually, Headmaster Green would come looking for Edgar and Dr. Selleck.

Using Edgar's keys was a gamble; if they didn't work on the female barracks, he would have to come back and figure out a way to get Hilda's keys, and during that time the two dead people in the office might be discovered. However, confronting both of the remaining staff members was an even bigger risk. Jonah had never been in a fight in his entire life; he would need a weapon, something he was familiar with, if he was going to stand a chance.

He got to his feet, walked over to Edgar's corpse—while circumventing the semicircle of blood surrounding Edgar's caved-in head—and unsnapped a metal ring bulging with keys from the dead man's belt. Jonah lifted Edgar's limp arm and gathered the baton and flashlight from the floor next to the body. The two heavy objects, particularly the baton, had inflicted much pain on him over the years, and he knew exactly how to use both of them. As he tried the weight of the baton in his hand, something on the floor snagged his eye.

One of the large needles next to Dr. Selleck's arm was still full of orange liquid. It was a large dose, even bigger than the one Edgar used to knock out the inmates. An ironic smile spread across Jonah's face.

* * *

8:19 P.M.

Headmaster Green licked his thumb and paged through a pile of papers, searching for a number. He stood facing his shuttered window, intently looking down at a file of reports that was laid across his desk, unaware that the door to his office was silently swinging open behind him.

His lip curled in disdain as a guitar solo echoed through the hallway. Hilda's music was annoying, but for now he would just deal with it. The schedule had been rough on the staff lately, so it was better to let her blow off some steam. Closing the office door wouldn't help; he would have to listen to her playlist of vintage garbage either way.

Keeping the office door propped open was an old habit, a trick he used to monitor the inmates during free study in the nearby classroom. Somehow, keeping the door cracked open deterred them from misbehaving; now he did it because he was just used to leaving it open.

Jonah silently stalked toward Headmaster Green, holding Edgar's baton in one hand and the needle up and ready in his other, his mind sharpened by a meaningful purpose—and red pills. With the Headmaster gone, he could break Barry out of the barracks, and then they could kill Hilda together.

Headmaster Green leaned back from the report and absently groped for a nearby vodka bottle. As he poured a fresh drink into his glass, his attention drifted back to the report. He picked up the glass, took a long drink, and put it aside.

Jonah stepped within striking distance just as Headmaster Green leaned forward on his desk with both hands. In surreal slow motion, he stabbed the needle as hard as he could into the Headmaster's neck, just below his hairline, and pumped orange liquid into it.

"What the… hell!" the Headmaster shouted as he groped for the needle. He spun around, finding Jonah staring back at him, and collapsed to the floor, knocking over a table and a lamp in the process. Jonah watched with curiosity as Headmaster Green managed to dislodge the empty needle, the older man's face stricken with disbelief.

"You fuckin' little…" His words trailed off as he fought the urge to pass out. He rolled to his belly and tried to claw his way forward.

Jonah's hand tightened around the baton as he looked down at the panicking, vulnerable individual who had doled out more beatings than he could count. He raised the baton and clenched his teeth as the polished oak club crashed down on the Headmaster's slippery skull. An urge to keep going overcame him, and he gave in to it, inflicting punishing blow after blow until Headmaster Green wasn't moving anymore. The maiming hail of malevolence purged feelings of hatred and helplessness, and served as retribution for years of violent beatings.

He dropped the baton and looked down upon the Headmaster's bloody body as violent impulses waned. Jonah realized in that moment that he was no longer a prisoner—he was a free man.

Numb, he staggered out, leaving Headmaster Green and the rigid rules of camp behind forever. He walked back into Dr. Selleck's office, squatted down to gather the bag of pills from the floor, and then turned his head, looking directly into the doctor's dead eyes. If it weren't for the five red pills he had gotten with his broccoli, he wouldn't be standing here right now.

"Goodbye, Dr. Selleck," he said to the pale, lifeless face that stared off into the afterlife. Now at peace with the doctor's passing, Jonah exited the office, ran as fast as he could manage down the hallway, and bolted through the front door.

He had to make the doctor's sacrifice worth it.

CHAPTER 19

Luckily, Jonah had quickly figured out how to operate Edgar's flashlight. The sky was cloudy and extraordinarily dark, and seeing anything outside without the light was difficult. He held the light on the large ring of keys as he flipped through them, trying each one sequentially on the lock to the men's barracks. He accidentally dropped the keys, which jingled as they bounced off the wooden door. As he bent to pick them up, he heard something move through the shrubs on the other side of the west fence. He slowly stood up and searched the blackness with squinting eyes.

A large shape suddenly pushed its way through forest overgrowth, uprooting trees and smashing branches as it brachiated out of the shadows and onto the gravel road that encircled camp. Veiled by the night, and standing less than a hundred yards from the men's barracks, the animal made deep, guttural breathing sounds, which were followed by sharp, angry snorts. Seemingly disturbed by what it smelled, the enormous creature leaned back on its stubby legs, straightened its spine, and raised itself up to a height that nearly rivaled the guard towers. Columns of steam poured from of its mouth as it let out a terrifying roar that shook the ground and resounded through the night air for miles in every direction.

As its lungs deflated, the roar became a piercing howl, which abruptly ended when the animal leaned forward and rested on its knuckles again. It began to brachiate up the gravel road, slowly creeping toward Jonah, as rustles and snapping branches in the depths of the forest echoed through the darkness; more animals were coming toward camp.

The inmates frequently heard similar outbursts after the sun went down, but strictly from within the safety of their cells. *Seeing* the beast roar, even while it was shrouded by the night, was an entirely different and very scary experience.

As the wind shifted, a putrid smell of carrion drifted into Jonah's nostrils. He turned back to the barracks door, fumbling with the flashlight and key ring, and resumed the tedious process of trying to fit a key into the padlock, this time with nervous, shaking hands. The animal wasn't behaving at all like the two others he had seen; in his experience, they appeared only for a moment and then ran off. This one, however, was getting closer with each passing second.

He dropped the key ring again, cursed, and picked it back up, having to start all over. He systematically went through the keys while keeping one eye on the fence. Humongous hands and feet crushed gravel as the animal suddenly charged up the road, brachiating onto the grass that ran parallel to the western fence, and then stopped twenty yards from where Jonah was standing.

Wispy clouds in the sky slowly thinned, and dim moonlight slipped through, revealing more of the creature. Jonah could see one bulbous eye protruding from under its misshapen brow; two sharp tusks as long as Jonah's body grew from its mouth; and the beast's pale, ghostly skin was marred with scars and burns. The animal sniffed the darkness, probing for a scent, and let out a deep, purring groan. It grabbed the chain links with a massive three-fingered hand and shook the fence, as if testing it for weaknesses.

Jonah tore his eyes from the animal and returned his focus to the lock. Halfway through the ring, he found one that worked; he threw the lock and chain to the ground and hurried inside the barracks.

He rushed down the hallway, stopped in front of Barry's door, and peered through the notch, seeing only darkness inside the cell. For a moment, he didn't know what to do next. "Barry!" he finally shouted.

"Jonah?" He heard Barry scramble to his feet and make his way to the door. A pair of disbelieving eyes appeared in the door notch. "You're... you got out?" he stammered, shocked by the unreality of it all.

Jonah paused, unsure of how to relate the evening's events. "They're dead," he said simply. He flipped through the keys, knowing that Barry's would be marked with a "23"; he had seen his number, and others, written on Edgar's keys before.

"Everybody?" Barry asked, confused.

"We need to go!" he shouted. "You said you would go with me, remember?"

"Yeah, I remember but..." Barry had never counted on Jonah being successful.

He found the key labeled with Barry's number and fit it snugly into the lock; the hasp unbolted, and Jonah swung the cell door open. Barry's eyes widened after Jonah stomped inside and clicked the cell bulb on. Jonah was covered in splatters of blood and held Edgar's flashlight and key ring. Best of all, he was carrying a huge bag of pills.

Jonah walked back out into the hall and leaned into Barry's doorway, waiting for him. "Come on!"

Barry shivered as he stood in place, shock overcoming him. Jonah slowly reached out and grabbed Barry's shoulder, comforting him. "Headmaster, Dr. Selleck, Edgar... are dead now. There's no reason to stay here anymore." He unsealed the bag of pills and dug into it, selecting five red pills from the bottom of the bag. "Take some of these—you'll feel better, trust me."

Barry grabbed his cup of water from the feeding table and washed the pills down. "Give me some orange too."

"Not until we get out."

"Why not?" Barry whined, offended. Jonah rolled his eyes and dragged Barry out of his cell and down the hallway.

As they exited the barracks, Jonah looked at the fence, searching for the animal, and was relieved to see that it had disappeared. Holding Barry by his uniform collar, he led them to the far side of the barracks, where they crouched under Charlie's shuttered window.

"Hilda's the only one left," Jonah said in a hushed tone. "She was in the administration building, in her bunk."

"Forget her!" Barry said loudly.

Jonah covered Barry's mouth with a bloodied hand. "Shhh!" he warned, and slowly released his hand. "I need to check for Arva," he said, motioning to the women's barracks. "I only have Edgar's keys. If they don't work, we have to kill Hilda."

Barry was violently offended by the suggestion. "No way!"

"Don't you want to rescue female 23?"

"Yeah, sure, it's just…" Other than fear and cowardice, Barry couldn't think of a reason to not kill Hilda and break the females out.

Hilda suddenly burst into the yard through the gate on the women's side of the yard, making Jonah and Barry flatten on the ground. She cried as she hurried toward the women's barracks, her sniffles and whimpers echoing through the yard. She held something that neither Jonah nor Barry had seen before, an oblong-shaped piece of metal that looked like a small hose, but with a handle. When Hilda disappeared around the back of the women's barracks, Jonah and Barry got to their feet, thankful that they hadn't been discovered.

"I need to see what she's doing." Jonah tried to get up, but Barry grabbed him by the shoulders.

"You're crazy!" he admonished in a hushed whisper. "She'll kill you!"

"I need to know what happened to Arva!" Jonah pulled away from Barry and strode across the yard toward the women's barracks without brave determination. Against Barry's better judgment, he tripped along after Jonah.

They wordlessly crossed the Lines of Division in parallel, venturing into the unknown side by side. Barry grinned. He had always wanted to know how the grass on the women's side of the yard felt under his feet. Jonah, on the other hand, was acting like crossing the Lines was no big deal. Something bad had happened; he could see it all over Jonah's face.

As they turned the corner of the women's barracks and walked toward the door, a loud, sharp bang erupted from inside, making them stop and crouch down. Seconds later, two more loud bangs were heard. Jonah approached the unchained door and put his ear to the wood, hearing faint sounds of crying coming from somewhere inside. Barry's eyes ballooned as Jonah pulled on the handle, opened the door, and slowly stepped inside the barracks. He took a deep breath and crept inside after Jonah, letting the door silently close behind him.

"You said you were just going to look!" he whispered angrily. Jonah put his index finger up to his closed lips, and then pointed around the corner of the hallway. Barry listened carefully; Hilda was talking to herself. Her mumbling, sniffles, and sobs eventually subsided… then she let out a long, drawn-out breath.

"I shouldn't be here right now, but here I am," Jonah and Barry heard Hilda say in a sharp, clear voice. "I used to be someone, a long time ago; now I'm just monster food, like you. What a fucking waste."

A deafening bang shook the barracks, making the two thin men cower against the ground. Jonah stood up and peered around the corner of the hallway. He leaned farther out and then turned back to Barry. "She's dead," he said matter-of-factly.

"How do you know?" Barry was still whispering for some reason. "Come see for yourself."

Barry stood up and followed Jonah to female 24's cell, the last one on the right; it was the only door that was wide open. From the doorway of the cell, Barry could see Hilda slumped over against the wall, on the floor near the inmate's bed. A large splash of blood and gray mush soaked the wooden boards behind her head.

Barry held his mouth and turned his back to the grisly scene, unable to look at it for another second. He quickly walked back to the entrance of the barracks and tried not to think about the closed door of his opposite number, female 23, the short girl with curly blond hair that he was supposed to marry one day. Her cell was only five feet away.

Barry paced over the worn floorboards, biting his long, filthy fingernails. Female 23's door was closed, but it wasn't locked. Sneaking a glance inside her cell would be easy; he just had to walk over there and open the door. Barry crouched down and fell back against the wall, hugging himself, rocking back and forth. He wanted to look inside, he really did, but if she resembled Hilda in her current state, it would take months, maybe years, to get the image out of his mind.

His stomach was getting jumpy from the red pills kicking in; any more excitement and he would probably throw up. He wrapped his arms around his legs and buried his face in his knees, resisting the urge to run back to his cell, go back to bed, and forget this night ever happened.

Jonah lingered in female 24's cell; Hilda wasn't the only dead person inside. The ugly girl that wore his number lay motionless on the ground, her left leg splayed over the excretion duct hatch. She had one bloody hole in her chest and another in her head. Her dead eyes stared at the ceiling, fragments from her skull littered the wooden floor, and a growing lake of crimson liquid was pooling underneath her.

As he stared at female 24's bloody face, he regretted the years he had spent being nauseated at the idea of marrying her. Forget her looks; she had been a prisoner too, and deserved better than dying on the floor of her cell. He backed out of the cramped room, ignoring Hilda's corpse altogether, and slowly shut the door. At least female 24 was free now.

He trudged through the barracks hallway, knowing that he was delaying the inevitable. Arva's cell was only two doors down; he felt compelled to look inside, even if he didn't like what he found. To his left, he found Barry curled into a ball, sitting on the floor next to the front door of the barracks.

"You OK?" he asked cautiously. He knew Barry was going through the initial shock of seeing a dead body and was dealing with the same harsh emotions that Jonah had endured the past twenty-four hours. But Barry had a softer soul and didn't cope with stress nearly as well as Jonah did.

"I want to look but I can't." Barry tilted his head upward. His eyes were red and swollen, his bony cheeks streaked with tears. He looked at female 23's door, fearing the worst. "If she's dead, I don't want to see."

Jonah nodded. "I'll look, then tell you."

"Thank you," Barry said, his trembling voice finally calming, "and not just for looking, for coming back for me."

Jonah bent down and patted Barry consolingly on the shoulder. "You're my best friend. I couldn't do this without you."

Barry managed a weak smile. Jonah spun toward female 23's cell and took a deep breath, preparing himself. Barry needed closure, just like he did. Arva's face and voice were still in his thoughts; they wouldn't go away until he found her.

He slowly swung the door open and peered inside the cell. Female 23 was lying on the floor near her window, her head cocked awkwardly to one side. A plate of peppers was splattered upside down next to her, partially covering her hand. A substantial portion of her head was missing; the upper-right corner of her face was a mass of pulpy carnage. A wave of nausea flooded into his stomach, making him turn away. He walked over to female 23's bed, reached up, and clicked the bulb off, then quickly exited the cell.

Barry watched Jonah shut female 23's door and released a lungful of anxious breath. With one shake of Jonah's head, her fate was communicated. Grief and sadness made new tears dribble down Barry's cheeks, but at least now he knew the truth. He wished he had known her real name.

Needles of apprehension spread through Jonah's chest as he took the final steps toward Arva's cell and stopped at her door. After one deep breath of confidence, he quickly opened the door and was confronted with darkness. He clicked Edgar's flashlight on and scanned the gloomy cell. The excretion duct hatch had been ripped off and was lying on the floor, her bed was empty and her blanket was missing, and a sticky, translucent substance stained the floorboards around the duct. She wasn't there; he didn't know if that was a good thing or not.

Jonah knelt down and carefully leaned on his hands, lowering his face to the floor. He sniffed the syrupy stain, which smelled like rotten earwax, in the desperate hope of finding a clue to Arva's whereabouts. Repulsed from the aroma, he began to pull away, but sounds coming from the open excretion hatch made him pause. He moved the flashlight beam inside the duct and peered in after it, the beam revealing a basement floor flooded with murky liquid and sludgy debris, and gray, featureless concrete walls. He removed the light and turned it off, then stuck his head through the opening of the excretion duct. He closed his eyes and concentrated on the echoing sounds, but they were too distant to clearly make out.

Even if Jonah had shined the flashlight directly on the creature lurking in the flooded basement directly below him, he still might not have seen it; the Master's green and brown scales blended in nicely with the clumps of sewage drifting in the murky water. The gruesome, reptilian humanoid silently stood up in the water, staring with hungry fascination at the flavored human head dangling down into its territory. Treacly drool spilled through the monster's fangs. Such a tasty treat this head of broccoli would be, it thought to itself.

"Jonah?" Barry called out, concern making his voice quiver.

Jonah withdrew from the opening and got to his knees. "I'm coming." He was sure he had heard some splashing noises and scraping sounds nearby, but chasing after faint, unintelligible sounds was just a big waste of time.

Frustrated, he stood up and tried to click on the lightbulb above Arva's bed, but the bulb was dead. He activated the flashlight and moved the beam of light throughout the cell, making sure he hadn't missed anything. After the visual perusal concluded without any positive results, he walked out, shaking his head. The answer to the same question he kept asking himself was still unanswered. *Where was she?*

As the cell door creaked shut, Jonah didn't see the two glowing red eyes watching him through the excretion duct. The Master chomped its fangs together, angrily spewing saliva. The rules had been broken, and it had been denied its meal. It was time to wake the others.

***

10:55 P.M.

Jonah and Barry walked hurriedly across the yard, toward the women's south gate. The marriage hut lay mere yards from the other side of the gate; neither man knew what they were going to say to the happy couple inside it.

"What if they don't believe us?" Barry spat, his breathing sharp and heavy. Jonah's dose of red pills was wearing off, but the drugs Barry had taken were going full throttle.

"They have no choice," Jonah replied grimly. As the gate swung open, he glanced at the sky, where he saw two pale circles gleaming down upon them. Mitch was right after all, Jonah mused—there were two moons.

"Hey, look, it's an animal!" Barry said enthusiastically, and pointed to the west fence. "And there's more, see?"

Three hulking creatures silently monitored the inmates through the fence, seemingly agitated as they roamed alongside it. Jonah recognized the animal with one eye; it was the same beast that had roared at him earlier. It reached out and shook the fence, making the entire structure quiver, and let out a brief, annoyed howl.

Jonah pushed Barry through the gate and swung it shut behind them, stealing one last look at the animals as it closed. Their number had grown to four. "Something's wrong with the animals," he said nervously as he led Barry along the sidewalk. "I don't want to see what happens if they get inside."

As they arrived at the front door of the marriage hut, another animal roared in the distance, this time from the east side of camp. Key after key was tried in the lock as sounds of the exterior fence being shaken increased. Although Jonah still had faith in the fence, he knew it wouldn't be able to take much more.

Finally, a key worked. He unchained the door and rushed inside, with Barry quickly following. He slammed the door shut, wrapped the chain around the inside handle, and clicked the lock into place.

Jonah turned to find Richard and female 22 sitting side by side at their feeding table, their heads cleanly shaven down to the skin. Both were mortified at the presence of the two inmates. Half-eaten poultry dribbled out of Richard's gaping mouth.

"What are you doing?" Richard demanded angrily.

"Escaping," Jonah said coolly.

Barry nodded his head in agreement. "We want you to come with us, both of you," he said, and turned his eyes to female 22.

Richard grabbed her hand, marking his territory, and puffed out his chest defensively. "Where's—" he started, his thoughts chaotically damming all at once.

"Dead," Jonah finished. "All of them; there's only us now."

Sue and Richard exchanged horrified glances. "But we just got married," Sue said innocently, not understanding the gravity of the situation.

"Monsters took Charlie, Richard. I saw him get taken; they're real. And right now, animals, big ones, are trying to tear down the fence!"

"No," Richard shot back, affronted by their invasion of his private time. "Charlie got magic slippers, like Headmaster Green said, and I don't care about the animals! The fence will keep them out! That's why they built it, stupid."

"You don't understand—they'll come for both of you now, either through the fence or up from the basement. You have to follow us!" Jonah said desperately.

Richard defiantly placed his arm around Sue and drew her in closer. "We're married now. We talk to each other and do other stuff too—secret stuff," he bragged. Sue put her hand on his and smiled at him. "We're staying," Richard said affectionately to Sue.

Sickened by Richard's attitude, Jonah rubbed his face and looked around the room, his eyes eventually falling on the hatch to the excretion duct. He dropped Edgar's ring of keys on the floor and walked over to the excretion duct, considering his next steps carefully. If he went down, there was no going back. Even if the little machines inside his body went off when he crossed the fence line, like Dr. Selleck said they would, getting around the animals or, even worse, fighting the animals weren't practical options. The basement was the only way.

Jonah unlocked the excretion duct hatch, flipped it back, and looked down into the stinky abyss. Barry, Richard, and Sue watched nervously, all wondering if Jonah would go through with it.

"Assigned food, exercise, pills, punishment… none of those things matter anymore," Jonah said, staring into Richard's eyes. "Everyone is dead. You will be too, if you don't leave with us." He twisted his legs together and fed them into the duct, then pushed the bag of pills downward, letting it drop and splash into the darkness below. He shimmed his slight waist past the edges of the duct, and then eventually got his shoulders through. Jonah's arms extended, with only his fingers left clinging to the familiarity and safety of Cydonia 6. Barry, Richard, and Sue held a collective breath. When Jonah's fingers let go, none of them could believe what they had witnessed.

Barry rushed over to the duct and looked down; Jonah was slowly getting up off the ground. Barry sat on the floor, pushed his legs together, and slowly wriggled through the duct. Before letting himself down, he looked back at Richard and Sue, and smiled. "Good luck," he said reluctantly, and dropped through the duct.

What felt like a sack of bricks hit Jonah in the back, throwing him down to the muddy, filthy ground. Barry had landed right on top of him, almost crushing him to death. The two men spit out disgusting, watery sludge as they got to their feet. They looked up, finding Richard staring down at them.

"Last chance, Richard," Jonah said as he wiped foul-smelling muck from his face. Richard almost said something, but instead he just slowly closed the hatch. They never saw each other again.

Barry fished the flashlight out of the water and clicked the beam on, shining it in Jonah's face. Jonah cringed back, covering his eyes. "Sorry," Barry said with a smirk.

"Point it around us," Jonah said condescendingly.

Barry scanned their surroundings, a nondescript, ten-foot high, rectangular concrete tunnel that disappeared into the darkness ahead of them. A tall wall of cinderblocks barred the way behind, leaving only one way to go. The flashlight splashed across a large number "5" that was painted on the wall to their right; Jonah recognized the symbol, which triggered a memory of Dr. Selleck counting on his fingers—one, two, three, four, five. He hoped the number was a good omen; they needed all the help they could get.

"This is where the monsters live," Jonah whispered to Barry. "Only talk if you have to." Barry nodded, and the two men began walking, feeling their toes squish in putrid mud with each step.

The flashlight beam bounced from the walls to the water and to the ceiling, eventually coming to stop on a shredded pair of inmate uniform pants that was floating on top of the ankle-deep sludge. Jonah waded toward the pants and picked them up, examining them; unable to find a number patch, he dropped the pants and motioned for Barry to move ahead.

As they wandered along the passageway, the smell of the air began to change to a bitter, rotten aroma. Suddenly, Jonah felt an enormous expanse all around him; the tunnel had widened into a massive underground chamber of unknown proportions. Dripping water echoed distantly; the air was grotesquely rancid with the stench of moldy death. Walking through would be wandering blind in a maze of putrefaction.

The two men stood at the mouth of the chamber, afraid to venture in farther. Neither could see the other side of the huge room, even with the aid of the flashlight, but they had to pick a direction or else stand there forever.

Barry swept through the nearby darkness with the narrow beam. Along the wall to their left, the light came across an uneven ramp of rubble that led up to a roughly hewn hole in the concrete wall. Dirt and stones had spilled out from the hole and lay mounded underneath it.

Jonah forced himself to walk farther out into the foul water, which became deeper at an alarming rate. He passed the rubble and the hole as the water reached his knees. "Come on!" he hissed to Barry, who reluctantly followed.

As the two former prisoners progressed deeper into the chamber, they found more tunnels branching off ahead. The space they were walking through was a gigantic intersection of dark passageways and mysterious cavities surrounded with debris. Above the professionally finished tunnels, the two men found painted numbers, some marked with two digits. Interspersed between these tunnels were roughly cut dirt corridors, much taller than their man-made counterparts, as if giant ants had burrowed into the vast chamber from the outside.

Nearby, to their left, the flashlight reflected off of a heap of bloody plastic. Jonah found some courage and slowly plodded closer to the plastic, curious yet fearful of the smudged shapes shrouded behind it. He peeled back layers of plastic until he found hair. With a shaking hand, Jonah pulled the top layer off, revealing Arva's severed head. A large bite had been taken out of her cheek and the stump of her neck, but he knew it was her by the eyes.

The image overwhelmed him; he fell ass-first into the sludge and sucked in sharp breaths of gross-smelling air.

"What is that?" Barry waded through the water, the flashlight beam glittering off of Arva's vacant eyes.

"It's Arva," Jonah said, as he pushed himself to his feet.

"Oh," Barry said softly, stopping in his tracks, knowing exactly what his friend was going through. He walked parallel to the wall, giving Jonah some space.

Other objects were hidden within the layered nest of translucent plastic; Mitch or Charlie could be in there somewhere, Jonah thought, as chills shot up his spine. He covered Arva's head again and took two steps back. Standing here now, out of the confines and rules of camp, he realized how little he knew about her.

The flashlight beam suddenly changed directions, leaving him in the dark. Jonah heard Barry make a panicked gasp.

"Jonah," Barry's voice trembled.

"Coming." He waded through the mud until he was standing at Barry's side.

The light was illuminating another floating object, this time a thin human arm. Chunks of connective tissue at the top half of the arm bobbed in the murky water; two of the arm's fingers were missing, and flesh had been torn away at the elbow. Barry shook with dread, making the flashlight quiver over the floating appendage.

Jonah's gaze drifted from the arm to the far wall and to an amorphous silhouette that began to move. He gently wrapped his hand around the flashlight that Barry was holding and turned it toward the distant figure. A tall, scaly creature was lying prone against the far wall, its legs drifting lazily in the sludgy water.

The basic shape of its head resembled a human's, but with a pig-like snout for a nose and misshapen fangs that crisscrossed inside its elongated mouth. Bloody intestines and organs floated next to its sleeping body, presumably the remnants of a meal recently concluded. The creature inhaled deeply and shifted its weight, searching for comfort. A long tongue flicked out from behind its fangs, and a vulgar smell belched out from its mouth.

A dreadful shriek resounded distantly through the gloomy catacombs, and suddenly Jonah thought he saw movement and activity everywhere. Splashing noises from the opposite end of the chamber were slowly growing in volume; all of the monsters must be waking up.

The creature sleeping nearby snorted and rolled on its side, shimmying in the mud and silt, the entrails floating in the water beside it undulating as the Master gradually found a comfortable position.

Barry shuddered as he began to mentally collapse, the flashlight beam bouncing in his shivering hand. Jonah grabbed Barry's face, not allowing him to succumb and shut down, and took the flashlight out of his hand. With one curling finger, Jonah silently ordered Barry to follow.

Jonah retraced their steps back to where they had entered, shining the light on the numbers above the tunnels along the way. He veered left, guiding them through chest-deep water and ankle-deep muck, and leading them across the huge expanse of the darkened chamber. They trudged straight through the middle of the reeking sewage, with the water level slowly subsiding, until they emerged along the far wall of the chamber near a concrete tunnel. Above the tunnel, Jonah found a painted number he didn't recognize.

Covered in putrid mud and shaking from the cold water, he pointed the flashlight down the passageway and found it blocked by a cave-in. Frustrated, he breathed out and pointed the light at their feet. "We have to find another one," he whispered to Barry.

Barry didn't react, his face stricken with shock. Jonah pulled him by the hand, hurriedly leading him along the wall, his free hand keeping the flashlight beam steady, and pointed it down to limit brightness. Hisses, splashes, and growls were now reverberating throughout the chamber, the noises gathering as a storm cloud above them. They needed to find a passageway soon, or they wouldn't have a chance.

Jonah abruptly tripped and fell forward into the mud with a loud, splashing thud. He scrambled to his feet, collecting the bag of pills and flashlight from the stinking water, and clicked the light off. Knowing he had given away their position to the creatures stalking them, he grabbed Barry's shoulder and sped off into the void ahead, his free hand glued to the concrete wall, feeling his way through the darkness. They raced forward, doubling their previous pace, as menacing sounds on their flank steadily increased; the hunt was on.

Jonah's hand suddenly whiffed through emptiness, indicating that they were next to a tunnel; he clicked the flashlight on and scanned the depths of the passageway. To his relief, the light shined on a painted number "5."

"Number 5, the same one we came in on the other side, and it's clear." He turned the light off, shoved Barry through the tunnel entrance, and snatched one last glance into the large chamber, where he saw groups of glowing red eyes moving through the darkness. Luckily, they weren't coming his way. Instead, the monsters were gathering along the far wall, near the tunnel that led back under the marriage hut. Unknown to Jonah or Barry, the sewage in which they were covered had masked their scent; the Masters were tracking two flavored humans, not the smell of decay and feces.

Jonah turned away from the chamber and tiptoed across the concrete floor of the tunnel until he was next to Barry. He moved his hand over the end of the flashlight and clicked it on. A dim ring of light around his palm provided enough brightness so that he could see Barry. Jonah could tell that his best friend was about to snap.

"Monsters are out there, a group of them, near the part of the basement we came out of," Jonah said icily. Barry began to shake, a whimper building in his chest. "They're not coming this way, but we have to be quiet so they don't hear us," he assured soothingly. Barry nodded, tears streaking down his face. "We walk slowly." Jonah clicked the light off and started down the tunnel.

Barry crept along behind Jonah, trying not to freak out. He didn't know where he was, he couldn't see, and monsters were somewhere out there, looking for him. He really, really needed some orange pills right now.

The men blindly felt their way through the passageway at a frustrating pace, the mushy surface beneath their feet slowly becoming drier as time went on. After what seemed like an endless period, Barry squeezed Jonah's shoulder, stopping him.

"You should put the light on now—I think we're safe."

"I think we need to go farther," Jonah whispered back.

"How much farther?" Barry asked, annoyed.

"I don't know, just farther, OK?"

Barry's silence meant he had grudgingly agreed. They resumed inching through the tunnel without a clue as to how far the passageway went.

CHAPTER 20

Sweaty and groggy, Richard rolled off of Sue, floating in emotions and sensations he'd never known existed. The two had become close companions almost instantly. Minutes after waking up in the marriage hut the day after the feast, they exchanged names and then removed their clothes to see what the other looked like naked. Both inmates were shocked at the differences, particularly the bodily features (or lack thereof) on their chests and between their legs. Richard then proposed that they rub their bodies together to see what happened, and boy, did something happen.

From then on, they repeated a physical ritual that ended almost as quickly as it began. After an explosion of incredible sensations and release of a newly discovered bodily fluid, Richard would feel sleepy and happy at the same time. Time would pass, and they would engage in the ritual again.

Richard swung his legs out of the bed, letting Sue, a name he had fallen in love with, wrap herself up in the oversized burlap blanket. He was famished and knew exactly what would cure his hunger: some poultry. He got up and strolled over to the feeding table, where he selected strips of pale chicken from the plate, shoving them all in his mouth at once. Grinning, he took two more pieces and added them to the wad of chicken in his mouth. It couldn't get any better than this.

A sharp, loud bang suddenly pounded against the excretion duct hatch, a violent sound that made Richard almost choke on the poultry he was swallowing. He nervously hurried over to the hatch, looking down upon it as he chewed.

Seemingly in reaction to the noises coming from the basement, extraordinarily violent reverberations rapidly began to unfold somewhere in the distance outside the marriage hut. An apocalypse of crashes, slashes, groans, and bellows melted together in an auditory soup of chaotic destruction, making Richard spin toward the door of the hut and forget the excretion duct hatch altogether. Jonah had said animals were out there, trying to rip down the fence. It sounded like they had just succeeded.

Sue sat up in bed and curled into a ball, shaking with fear, her head spinning as the direction that the sounds were coming from quickly changed. Richard felt helpless; he scurried to the door and pressed his ear against it. The noises of annihilation were coming from somewhere out in the yard, as if everything were being torn down, including the barracks and guard towers.

A mighty quake shook the ground as an unseen structure tumbled, almost knocking Richard off his feet and making the walls of the marriage hut shudder. The booming sound was quickly followed by a choir of unearthly, beastly roars. As if competing with the distant sounds of encroaching devastation, another bang pounded against the excretion duct hatch, and then another; whatever was down there now urgently wanted in. Richard ran back over to the hatch and stared at it, too afraid to touch it.

"Jonah!" Richard shouted down at the hatch. "Is that you?" he asked warily, his voice strained with terror. The excretion duct hatch jostled as something heavy slammed against it. The thin wood panel was on its last legs; only one flimsy screw now kept it shut.

Richard ran over to the bed and huddled with Sue, shaking and cringing from the pandemonium. Destruction was steadily making its way into the administration area from the yard, while something from below was about to destroy the excretion duct hatch, leaving Richard and Sue caught in the middle.

A sudden impact on the door of the marriage hut sent tremors through the entire structure, splitting the thick wood down the middle. The steel chain wrapped around the interior handles of the door strained from the powerful collision, nearly breaking. Richard held Sue as tightly as possible, tears streaming from his eyes.

Across the room, the hatch exploded from the top of the duct, bounced off the wall, and landed by the feeding table. Two scaly brown hands reached up through the hatch; long, thin arms followed; then its head appeared. Two red eyes looked menacingly at Richard and Sue, who flung themselves under the burlap blanket.

A snout dripping with mucus snorted twice as it analyzed the unfamiliar atmosphere of the hut. Some of the surrounding smells were not to the Master's liking, and the room was too bright, but the aroma of flavored humans was excessively hard to resist. It pushed itself up into the hut, having to brace its thin frame against the floor as its long legs slid through. Foul-smelling mud and syrupy drool splattered the floor as it came to a hunched stand, the short ceiling preventing it from rising to full height.

Another set of long, reptilian arms stretched through the hatch, and a second Master joined the first inside the marriage hut, but it was shorter, with warts growing from its snout, and its scales were speckled with green spots. As a third attempted to breach the hatch from the basement, the green-spotted Master lashed out at it and hissed, bubbles of gooey spittle spilling out in the process.

Thuds against the marriage hut door continued as the taller Master smashed the lightbulb above the doorway with a clawed fist, leaving only the dim bulb above the bed to illuminate the small room. Annoyed, the hideous creature let out a booming growl, which instantly calmed the activity outside the door. A claim had been made; no others could taste these two dishes now.

In tandem, the deformed, reptilian humanoids stalked the shivering human mass that lay beneath the burlap blanket. The green-spotted Master stretched out its claws and inhaled deeply through its warty snout. "Poultry," it said in a low-pitched growl, then sniffed the air.

"And ssselery… yesss," the taller Master's tongue flicked out under its snout.

"Go away!" Richard shrieked from under the blanket.

Instead, both creatures stepped in closer. "Time to eat," the green-spotted Master moaned.

* * *

1:26 A.M.

Walking through darkness had made time disappear. It wasn't until Jonah and Barry heard shrill screams echoing through the tunnel behind them that the men noticed each other again. Frightened eyes sightlessly searched through the gloomy tunnel; Jonah clicked the light on, making the distance disappear, leaving only the bright area around them visible. Suddenly, louder, more ferocious screams accompanied a series of raging growls, which were followed by sounds of mayhem and violent slaughter. Although Jonah and Barry couldn't see what was happening, they both knew that Richard and Sue had just met their end. The event triggered an identical reaction from both of them: flee.

Jonah and Barry ran as quickly down the tunnel as their legs and bare feet would take them, the flashlight flickering against the walls of the tunnel as Jonah's arms flailed beside him. It didn't take long for the two skinny former prisoners to run out of gas. After all, they hadn't eaten since yesterday, and neither was conditioned for running—it was an activity that the staff of Cydonia 6 thoroughly discouraged.

They walked in silence with the flashlight remaining on, too tired and traumatized to talk to each other. Jonah cradled the bag of drugs in his arms as he staggered forward, cracking it open once in a while to recharge their fading energy with red pills. After a while, even the red pills weren't working.

"I need to stop," Barry finally said somewhere behind Jonah, his voice fatigued to the point of collapse. Jonah turned the flashlight beam on Barry, who looked dead on his feet. Barry waved the light away, irritated.

"OK, we can take a break, but just for a little bit." Jonah clicked the light off, dropped the pills next to him, and leaned back against the tunnel wall, sliding slowly to the floor. He was asleep before his backside hit the cement.

* * *

3:41 A.M.

Vibrations shook him awake, then spikes of pain shot through his head. Headmaster Green groaned and breathed in, his vision gradually returning. A lamp was lying sideways on the floor, its bulb still lit. Slowly, he realized where he was—on the floor of his office. Moving was almost impossible, but he forced himself to roll over until his face pointed up toward the ceiling. Broken ribs, pulverized muscles, and a shattered skull made the task unbearably painful. He grimaced ironically. Jonah had worked him over good.

Tingles of fear swallowed his pain the second he noticed that the hatch into the basement had been torn off at the hinges, leaving no barrier between him and the Masters below. His desk had been shoved aside and now sat crookedly against the wall. Something (or things) had come up from below. Panic and adrenaline swept through him; he unsuccessfully tried to sit up, and shrieked, having to fall back down to nullify the agony.

Floorboards creaked as heavy steps shifted over the ground. With dread surging through every nerve in his body, Headmaster Green turned his head sideways, looking under his desk, where he found two large, brown, scaly feet. "Please, don't do this," he begged, and spun painfully to his stomach, hoping the Master would somehow magically vanish. Ignoring his request, it stomped around the corner of the desk, slowly stalking him.

Headmaster Green crawled on his stomach, away from the open hatch and the monster that was hunting him, desperately trying to reach the door to his office. He knew it didn't matter, but he had to try, even though the door looked a million miles away. Throbbing pain shot through his chest as broken bones in his ribcage ground together, making him flop to the ground and instantly halt all progress. The Headmaster rolled to his back again and leaned against the wall, frantically searching through plausible arguments for staying alive. "Just wait a second, I can explain—this wasn't my fault!"

"Greedy," the tall Master bellowed, its red eyes analyzing the bloody human cowering before it. He smelled like grease and alcohol, but would surely make a delicious meal.

"You need me," Headmaster Green whimpered, then suddenly shouted, "You need me!"

A crooked smile curled around the fangs of the Master as it slowly shook its head. "Not anymore," it purred, and braced itself against the wall, preparing for the first bite.

"You need me!" Headmaster Green shouted through tears, the words quickly cut off as razor-sharp teeth simultaneously punctured his throat through his Adam's apple and bit through the crown of his skull. He heard a distant crunch, a sound that echoed vacantly; as his life faded, a vision of Jonah standing over him appeared in his mind's eye.

The Master thrashed against the Headmaster's lifeless body,

chomping through bones and organs, as one thought repeated through Headmaster Green's dimming consciousness: *I wonder where Jonah is right now.*

* * *

6:11 A.M.

Jonah's eyes blinked open; dim light was bathing the cement directly in front of his face. He lifted his head and turned toward the source of the light, which was so far down the tunnel that he couldn't clearly see where it was coming from.

Aching muscles fought back against the motions he began to put himself through as he got to his feet. Barry was asleep on the ground a few feet behind him. Jonah hoped he didn't look as terrible and filthy as his friend, but odds were he looked even worse.

His mouth was parched; he couldn't remember the last time he wanted water so badly. He stretched his back, making it pop, and kicked Barry's foot, waking him.

"Huh?" Barry rubbed his eyes with his dirty hands. "Where are we?"

"Still under the ground, but there's light up ahead, maybe a way out," Jonah croaked. He tried to swallow, but his tongue was too dry. He surveyed the light at the end of the tunnel as he retrieved the smudged bag of pills from the ground. "It looks far, but it's better than going back."

Barry pushed himself off the ground and disjointedly got to his feet. "I want water, real water, not shit water like back there."

They shuffled toward the light, wincing and shifting along the way. All of the walking and running they had done during the night had ruined their lower bodies. Waking up, and having to walk even more, felt like torture; each step sent spikes of pain up their thin legs.

Jonah tiredly looked at the plastic bag of pills as he trudged forward. His body was telling him that he needed to take some orange, and maybe some red for good measure, but ingesting anything right now but water simply wasn't possible.

Each aching step toward the dull light brought more clarity to their immediate destination. At the end of the passageway, a concrete shaft tall enough to climb through arced upward at a steep incline. It took eons, but Jonah and Barry's bruised, swollen feet eventually stepped off of the concrete floor and onto a bed of soft leaves and gritty orange dirt that had amassed at the bottom of the shaft.

Jonah peered up the inclining tunnel and smiled. "Daylight," he said wistfully, his eyes soaking in the natural light pouring down the shaft. After hours of slogging his way through darkness, he wanted the sun on his face almost as much as he wanted water in his stomach.

"Let's go!" Barry blurted impatiently.

Jonah stuffed the bag of pills down his pants and tucked in his shirt over the bulge to secure it as he made his ascent. With the flashlight in one hand, he braced himself against the sides of the shaft and climbed up into it, having to bend forward as he progressed upward to prevent himself from slipping back down.

Barry awkwardly mimicked Jonah's body positioning and followed him up the inclining passageway. As the grueling climb went on, dust and dirt particles fell into his nostrils, making him suddenly sneeze. Jonah jumped from the noise and quickly reached back, grabbing Barry's tattered burlap uniform top, keeping him stable. If either of them fell down the shaft from their current position, some bones would certainly be shattered, or worse. Barry sneezed two more times, his breathing gradually calming after the second outburst. Jonah waited to make sure the fit had concluded before resuming his trek up through the shaft. The two tired, skinny men were almost crawling by the time they made it to the top.

A colorful, magical vision slowly began to coalesce as Jonah and Barry got closer to what they now knew was the end of the shaft. The former prisoners grinned as wonderful smells, sounds, and sights poured into their senses. Moments later, the men emerged into warm sunshine, thoroughly exhausted and breathing heavily. The found themselves standing on plush green grass and shaded by a vast canopy of trees. Jonah giggled, unable to fully fathom the foreign experience.

"Ha-ha-ha!" Barry shouted, and ran over to a tree, hugging it, feeling its warm, rough texture against his skin. "I never thought I would get to touch a tree." He flopped down on the ground and covered himself in brown leaves, laughing to himself.

Jonah wandered through brilliantly colored bushes and trees, his feet cushioned by soft grass. He couldn't see a fence anywhere, and it was a joyous experience. Curious, he turned and examined the tunnel from which they had emerged, wondering what it looked like from the outside. The shaft was cut into the bottom of a tall hill dotted with shrubs and small trees; as Jonah's concentration sharpened, a familiar sound began to stand out from the wind that was rustling through the forest. "Hey, come here!" he shouted to Barry.

Barry walked up behind him, brushing off his uniform. "You should try covering yourself in leaves—it feels really great!"

"You hear that?" Jonah asked softly, and cocked his head toward the sound. The two men listened carefully, both hearing a steady trickling noise somewhere in the distance. "It sounds like running water, like in Dr. Selleck's sink," Jonah said, and licked his liquid-starved lips.

They walked through the trees, following the sounds of moving water until they found it—a four-foot-wide stream that ran down from the hills and through the forest. Upon seeing it, Jonah broke into a run, which quickly became a limp. Barry sped by and threw himself on the ground next to the stream, where he gulped down water by the handful. To one-up Barry, Jonah plunged his entire head into the water and ingested greedy mouthfuls of the soothing fluid until his belly felt like it would pop. After their insides were taken care of, the men washed tunnel-sludge from their faces, hands, and arms, and then lay on the ground, feeling exhausted and rejuvenated at the same time.

"What do we do now?" Barry asked as he looked up into the sky.

Jonah was just asking himself that exact same thing. "We know the tunnel that we came out of goes right back to camp, so we go away from the tunnel."

Barry eventually followed Jonah's line of reasoning and nodded, "Right."

"So I was thinking we follow the water. It's going the right way, and we can drink as much water as we want."

"I…" Barry hesitated. "I want some orange pills now."

"Me too, but let's also take some red. We can't fall asleep out here."

"OK!" Barry said voraciously, and dug into the bag of pills.

"Not too many—Doctor Selleck said we could die," Jonah warned sternly.

"Really?" Barry said, shocked, and Jonah slowly nodded. Barry breathed out, perturbed. Even out here, someone was controlling his pills. "Then how many can I take?"

"Three orange, three red?" Jonah proposed.

"How many is three?" The calculation stumped him, but suddenly he had a solution. "I get four brown, back… back in the cell," he finished awkwardly. "So maybe we take four of each? I can count those."

"We'll make it four, then."

Barry divided up the pills, and they quickly consumed them. Satiated with water and not yet feeling numb from the opiates, they resumed their trek, this time following the course of the stream. Jonah quickly discovered that walking alongside moving water was a tranquil experience. If his legs and feet didn't feel like they were going to fall off, he would probably be enjoying the stroll through the forest. Once in a while they stopped for a drink, and he soaked his feet and legs in the cool water, but eventually they had to start walking again. After a while, he began to doubt that the walking would ever end.

The trees gradually got smaller and more infrequent, and the sun slowly got lower in the sky. When the stream they had been following abruptly ended, they set off in a direction through the forest that seemed to align with their previous path, and hoped for the best. Wide fields of tall grass were now spread out before them; there still was no sign of anyone else.

CHAPTER 21

SEPTEMBER 16, 2335 M.E.
2:02 P.M.

As Jonah and Barry stomped through a field of particularly tall grass, something odd and seemingly random began to come into view. A thick black line made of crushed stone carved an even course through the grass, crossing their path perpendicularly, and disappeared into a cluster of tall trees to their right. Jonah crouched and touched the surface of the black line, finding it warm, dense, and composed of tiny black stones all crammed together.

"What do you think it is?" Barry asked skeptically.

"They kind of look like the small stones outside of camp, but they're even smaller, and black instead of the other colors. Headmaster Green called it 'the road.'"

"I'm tired of walking through that grass; it's cutting my feet," Barry whined.

"Then we'll follow the black line and see where it goes," Jonah said absently. At this point, he didn't care which direction they went. They had to find shelter soon, or they would be sleeping out in the open. The two tired men trudged along the smooth black line, a sunlight-warmed surface wide enough for eight people to walk side by side.

Barry was stumbling along with his head down, eyes on his feet, lost in dimwitted thoughts, so Jonah was the first to see it: a small green building the size of his cell, but tipped on its end, sat on the side of the road less than one hundred yards ahead. He stopped, grabbed Barry's shoulder, and pointed at it. Instantly nervous, they scuttled off the black line and hid behind the wide trunk of a nearby tree.

"I don't see anyone," Barry said fretfully.

Jonah didn't see anyone either. One side of the building was missing, so they could easily look inside. From this angle, through the trees, he could also see beyond the small building, where the black line ended at a sturdy steel gate. Towering green bushes and trees obscured just about everything else around the end of the black line. "We need to get closer so we can get a better look," Jonah said, then slowly crept through the trees hunched over, Barry five steps behind him.

They broke off from the cover of the trees and jogged to the small building, where they found a plastic chair and a moldy coffee mug inside. A metal box full of indecipherable buttons and switches hung on the wall. Small words were written on the box, but Jonah was in no mood to try to read right now. He turned and found Barry staring through the tall steel gate, his mouth hanging open. Whatever had captured his attention must be fascinating. "What's wrong?" he asked, concerned.

"You have to see this," Barry said, stricken with awe, and reached out to lean on the gate with both hands. Jonah walked out of the miniature, three-walled building, extremely curious as to what Barry was looking at. With his back now turned to the metal box, he couldn't see a small red light on the middle row of buttons suddenly blink on.

As he approached Barry, Jonah noticed that the steel gate was dented and distorted, as if something with immense strength had ripped it open. When he arrived next to his friend and fellow former inmate, what he saw took his breath away.

Contradicting Jonah's assumption, the black line didn't end at the gate; it continued past the steel barrier into a wide, grassy area, where it transformed into an ellipse. Looming above the black, oval line and the surrounding grass was the largest building Jonah had ever seen. His only frame of reference for a comparable building was the administration building at the transition camp where he had grown up, but that was just an incrementally larger version of the structure of the same name at Cydonia 6. The edifice he was looking at now was at least a hundred times bigger.

A behemoth of an L-shaped, four-story building took up two-thirds of the fenced-in compound. Sections of its slanted roof had caved in; glass windows were shattered, broken, or missing altogether; garbage and rubble spilled out from the ground-floor windows; veins of ivy and moss had consumed one entire exterior wall and were slowly infiltrating the other visible exterior walls.

To their left, interlocking, single-story buildings extended all the way from the black line to the far fence. Across the compound, to their right, was a diamond-shaped field of tall grass and thin trees. Grass had grown through, and overcome, rusty metal benches that fanned out in a semicircle along the edge of the grass. The mangled steel gate that Barry was leaning against was only a small section in a network of fencing that encompassed the entire compound. Bushes and trees grew in concentrated clumps along the entirety of the sturdy fence, camouflaging everything behind it with a far-reaching canopy of leaves, branches, and undergrowth.

Standing here at the main gate, Jonah could see that both doors to the ground-floor entrance of the immense building were wide open. They had a way in.

"Maybe it's where the guards live," Barry said coolly, as if reading Jonah's mind.

"No shutters on the windows. And this gate, the entire fence, doesn't look like what we had in camp," Jonah reasoned. "We need a place to sleep, and there might be food." He grabbed the misshapen gate and swung it open with ease. The two men stood there for a moment and then walked skeptically toward the giant building, their eyes not trusting the reality of such an intimidating structure.

* * *

2:44 P.M.

Jonah shifted on the mushy, moldy mattress he had found lying outside the entrance to the tall building, his buttocks finally resting on a section that didn't spear his backside with a sharp metal spring, and opened the bag of pills. He frowned at what remained of the pills; they were getting low.

Barry hadn't stopped staring into the entranceway of the building since they had decided to rest just outside of it. "Something smells really bad in there. And it looks too big to be real. I wonder how many rooms are inside."

Jonah shook his head, mildly annoyed; when Barry was nervous, he tended to voice every thought that sprang to mind. He separated groups of pills, using a smaller count than usual: three red and three orange. "Here's your pills," he said lightly, hoping Barry wouldn't notice the diminished dosage.

Barry's complaints suddenly vanished. He appeared in front of Jonah, his palm outstretched. Although they had no water to wash down the pills, both men joyously swallowed their allotment.

"Less than last time?" Barry asked innocently while gulping the pills down through a dry throat.

"We're running out." The statement was partially true. Plenty of brown and blue pills remained, but those colors didn't make you feel like red and orange pills did. A significant amount of their stockpile had been consumed during their endless walk through the dark tunnel. "Look through the building, see what's in there?"

"All right." Barry nodded; they both knew they needed a distraction from the pill predicament. In all truth, there was nothing else for them to do.

The foyer of the enormous building smelled stale and bitter. Trash, empty aluminum cans, and decaying drywall littered the ground. Jonah and Barry marveled over the individual pieces of refuse, the colors and images too alien for them to understand. The tide of garbage gave way to a wide hallway, which led to an architectural eccentricity that neither man could explain. A series of connected planks ascended up from the hallway, paving an even path to the next level of the dilapidated structure, and what looked like the upper levels as well. Stairs were a concept they couldn't grasp; never once had stairs been a subject of conversation, much less the topic of a classroom lesson.

"Can we walk on them?" Barry asked with a smile.

"I guess we have to!" Jonah giggled as he ran up the stairs and stood triumphantly atop the first landing.

Barry ran up the stairs, turned the corner of the landing, and charged up the next level of stairs, then abruptly slipped and fell on his face. He eagerly resumed his disorderly ascent as quickly as possible.

"Wait!" Jonah shouted and ran after him. A combined surge of red and orange pills had scuttled his tiredness; excitement and glee were now in firm control. They were free and in a wondrous new place. Living in the moment had never felt so good. Jonah's lung power died halfway up the second flight of stairs. He found Barry grinning and seated on the last step to the third story of the building. They wordlessly exchanged agreement on their next course of action as Jonah caught his breath. It was time to explore.

The narrow flashlight beam panned over the walls and the interiors of identical-looking rooms as they investigated the depths of the building. Edgar's light was somehow still working, but the power was getting low. They systematically checked each room on the third floor, finding all of them in the same condition—empty, except for a floor strewn with garbage. As they progressed down the hallway and scanned each room, Jonah's hopes for water and food began to dwindle.

At the end of the hallway, which took a while to reach, they found a closed door—the only closed door on the entire floor. A red sign consisting of two words adorned the door, but neither of them knew what "File Room" meant. Jonah turned the knob and slowly pushed the door open. A putrid smell of decay and human waste punched him in the face.

"Ewww," Jonah said, and covered his nose with his arm as he ventured in farther. Tall metal shelves standing in perfectly even rows lined a long, bowling alley–sized chamber that was void of windows. With the exception of loosely scattered papers, folders, and cardboard boxes, the shelves were empty.

Jonah absently dug into a box, picked up a random paper, and raised it to his face. The paper contained a grid of numbers, a topic he had no interest in trying to understand. He crumpled up the paper, threw it aside, and began rooting through another box.

Barry, holding his sleeve over his nose and mouth, busied himself by opening every closed door he could find. He found empty closet after empty closet, until he reached the last closet, on the far side of the room. The disgusting smell that swam out of the last closet's opening door made Barry's stomach lurch, but he held the vomit back, afraid of losing the sensations of the red and orange pills. Back in Cydonia 6, when he was forced to eat disgusting beef, he had refined the art of suppressing the urge to throw up. Edgar would always beat him extra-hard for ruining the floor with undigested food, so he had to learn how to control himself. At least here, no one was waiting to cave in his skull if he vomited.

The floor of the closet was caked in a dense layer of dried fecal matter. Fat green flies crawled all over the mound of black, crusty material as finger-long worms writhed through it. Barry slammed the closet door and leaned against it, concentrating on keeping the scant contents of his stomach in their current place. As his eyes opened, he noticed something unusual lying on the floor between the last two rows of metal shelves, at the far end of the room. Blankets were piled against the wall in a disorganized heap; two human-sized legs stuck out from under the blankets. "Hey, I found something!" he said loudly, his voice trembling.

Jonah was on the other side of the File Room, but from Barry's tone, he could tell it was important. He dropped a folder full of papers and raced toward him, finding the skinny man staring down the last aisle of metal shelves. Jonah traced Barry's line of sight; needles of ice coursed through his spine as his eyes came across the two legs jutting out from under the heap of blankets.

The men exchanged worried glances and then carefully walked toward the legs. Jonah bit his bottom lip as they neared the pile of blankets, holding the flashlight ready in case of an attack, but the legs hadn't moved, and the two former inmates were making plenty of noise along the way.

"I wonder who it is," Barry mused as he scratched an itch deep within his beard. "It could be a monster. If it's a monster, you have to kill it."

"Why do I have to kill it?" Jonah demanded.

"You killed the Headmaster," he said bluntly, as if Jonah should have known better.

Jonah gulped. Those events had been pushed to the back of his mind, but now they were crystal-clear. He didn't regret it, but he also didn't like thinking about it.

Only twenty yards away, details of the mysterious legs were becoming more discernable. They weren't wearing shoes, like the camp administrators (and Jonah assumed the guards) wore, so that was a plus. The thighs of the legs were covered by rolled-up burlap pant legs, but the thin, discolored lower legs could be seen.

Jonah and Barry stopped five feet from the pile of blankets, which turned out to be stuffed full of seat cushions and some kind of fluffy, white rectangular objects that they couldn't identify. Jonah's heart beat heavily in his chest as he stepped next to the legs and peeled a thick layer of blankets back, exposing a body beneath.

The stiff, decaying corpse of female 19 met their eyes. Still wearing her Cydonia uniform and numbered patch, she was lying on her right side, facing away from the wall. A dark, moldy stain spread out on the blanket underneath her mouth. Flaky brown skin stuck to the blankets in several spots. The knuckle and forefinger of her right hand were scarred and scabbed, covering a deep wound that had healed long ago.

"She escaped all right," Jonah said, the words weighing heavily on his mind.

Barry got to one knee, examining the corpse's hand. He pulled on the sleeve of female 19's uniform, lifting it off the ground, revealing a small pile of pale orange pills. "Look at all those pills!" he drooled greedily. "Give me the bag."

"They're like, years old!" Jonah admonished incredulously. "She escaped before we even got to camp—we can't eat those!"

"Why not?" Barry grabbed the pill bag from Jonah's hand, opened it, and dumped the pills inside.

Jonah pushed back more blankets and threw them to the side; a small treasure trove of supplies was uncovered: six and a half small bottles of water; and two full cans, and one empty can, of generic dog food. He quickly grabbed a water bottle and squeezed it. The plastic bent and then returned to its original shape, making him smile. Using his limited deduction skills, he examined the bottle closely and tried to poke his thumb through the plastic top. When this tack failed, he turned the top of the bottle clockwise with his thumb and forefinger, eventually prying it loose.

A popping sound dragged Barry's focus from the bag of pills to the cylindrical plastic container that Jonah was holding. Jonah sniffed the top of the opened plastic bottle, then tipped it back and gulped down clear liquid. "Hey! Where'd you get that?" Barry said angrily.

Jonah took a breath, momentarily saving the last third of the bottle, and handed Barry an unopened bottle from the floor. He resumed his frantic consumption of water until the last drop was on his tongue. Cool fluid trickled through his internal organs as it was absorbed, bringing a content feeling to his stomach. Meanwhile, Barry was struggling mightily with his bottle.

Jonah reached down and collected the remaining water bottles from the nest of blankets but quickly thought twice about the half-empty bottle. A hairy fungus was growing inside it; even the water at Cydonia 6 looked cleaner than that. He looked curiously at the colorful cans by his feet but quickly forgot them. Hugging the four unopened plastic bottles, he yanked the water bottle from Barry's discombobulated hands and unscrewed the cap. Before he could hand it back, Barry was guzzling liquid from it. Water splashed down his neck as he drank, the wide smile on his face preventing a comprehensive seal from forming. Jonah smiled too. Finding water was a much-needed stroke of good fortune.

"What did you find in the closets?"

"Shit," Barry said simply between gulps of water.

"Shit?"

Barry nodded, his cheeks bulging with liquid. He swallowed heavily and let out a gratified gasp. "It was all over the floor. I don't see any excretion ducts up here, and she had to go somewhere." Barry nodded at female 19's corpse.

Jonah shrugged, not wanting to personally investigate Barry's explanation. It already smelled bad enough in the large room. During one of many glances into the rotten face of female 19, his eyes snagged once again on the metal cans lying on the floor beside her. "Here," Jonah said as he handed Barry two water bottles, keeping the other two firmly protected, and squatted down next to the corpse. One of the words on the cans was familiar.

"Food," Jonah said, reading the word aloud.

"Where?" Barry blurted, his eyes opening wide with anticipation.

Jonah picked up the empty can and smelled it, the aroma making his nose wrinkle. He threw it to the floor and selected one of the two sealed cans, turning it in his hands. As his mind worked through the symbols written across it, he picked up the other can, which mostly resembled the first, but with slightly different writing. He stood up slowly, looking back and forth between the two unrecognizable objects. "Dog food," he said quizzically, knowing he had heard the words before. Suddenly he remembered. "Edgar called me a dog before he threw me in the hole, the last night in camp."

"Then what happened?" Barry asked, confused.

"Then he spit on me," Jonah said distractedly, his eyes studying the writing as words coalesced in his mind. "This one says beff, I think."

"You mean beef?" Barry was offended.

"This says chick-en." He handed the can to Barry, who cradled it uneasily.

"How do we eat it?" Barry asked, befuddled.

Jonah pondered the question carefully. He looked at the opened can, which was now on the other side of the aisle. The top of the can was curled back; a metal ring connected to the curled top was bent backward. He flipped the can in his hands upside down, then right side up, and noticed a similar-looking ring on the top of it, but the ring lay flush with the metal top. Jonah pried at it with his index finger, eventually cracking the metal top open.

Barry studied the process and repeated it on his can.

Jonah tugged at the ring; the top of the can easily pulled back, exposing a brown, jellified substance inside. He discarded the top, dropping it to the floor, and dipped his finger into the gloopy brown material. He excavated a small mound and cautiously smelled the chunks.

Barry popped the top off his can of chicken-flavored dog food and hesitated, wanting to see what Jonah would do next before he did anything else.

Jonah shoved his finger in his mouth. "Mmmm," he moaned, a burst of flavor filling his mouth.

Barry used three fingers to dig out brown, chunky material and shovel it into his mouth, ravenously consuming the pasty matter as wonderful tastes spilled down his esophagus.

"If she was eating this, there might be more," Jonah said through a mouthful of food.

"This is great!" Barry ecstatically scooped more dog food out of the can.

Jonah's eyes drifted to female 19's decomposed face. Barry was right, this was great, but after everything they had been through, things needed to turn out differently for them. This couldn't be the end of their story; he wouldn't let it be the end.

CHAPTER 22

Walking down the staircase was much more fun than walking up. Jonah particularly liked skipping the last few stairs and jumping onto the landing, even though sometimes it sounded like the wooden boards would collapse under his feet. His confidence in surviving the world outside of Cydonia 6 was growing, and for now it seemed that they had shelter. They just needed to find more food and water.

Feeling re-energized from the delicious dog food, the men decided to search the entire building, starting from the ground floor, and gather all the supplies they could get their hands on. As they reached the bottom of the stairs, a chilly wind blew in from the open entranceway, making them both shiver.

"Let's also look for blankets," Jonah said, his teeth chattering.

They turned left, walking away from the entrance and down a corridor that led into the depths of the ground floor, where the ceiling was much higher and the shadows much darker. Jonah clicked the flashlight on and scanned through the trash on the floor. All of the plastic bottles were empty; every single can was open and covered in black mold. Getting away from the entrance hadn't helped them warm up, either; it felt like cold air was coming toward them from the rear of the building too.

The hallway ended at a large, open room full of chairs and desks. Wide plastic viewing screens hung crookedly on the surrounding walls, the faces of which were all shattered; wires, computer parts, communication hardware, and other unidentifiable pieces of machinery lay strewn throughout the room. "What is all this stuff?" Barry asked as he picked up, and then quickly dropped, a splintered circuit board.

Jonah panned the light over mysterious hunks of metal and wires, and came across a discolored white chair riddled with bullet holes. "Hey, look at this." Jonah awkwardly rolled the white chair out from behind a caved-in desk and looked closely at it. Seven round perforations dotted the backrest; from the appearance of the holes, something had punched through the rear of the backrest and exploded through the front.

Barry stuffed his forefinger through one of the holes. "Goes all the way through," he declared, announcing the obvious yet again.

A glint on the floor caught Jonah's eye. He bent down and picked up two bullet shell casings; the long, bronze-colored metal shells were scattered all over this section of the floor. "They kind of look like small cans," Jonah said, bewildered as to what the metal objects might be, and handed one to Barry, who sniffed it.

"I don't think food was in there," Barry said, and dropped the shell among the wires and machinery.

"There has to be more food in here somewhere. We'll find it," Jonah said uneasily, struggling to convince himself not to give up hope. Finding a reliable, long-term source of food and water was critical. Without either, they would have to search for a new place to stay.

Jonah and Barry meandered through the expansive room, finding a growing number of shell casings on the floor as they progressed. On the far side of the chamber, they came across burn marks, collapsed walls, and massive craters in the concrete floor. Dark smudges stained the walls and ground; bullet holes punctured every surface within sight. Some kind of epic battle must have taken place where they were standing. They resumed exploring, turning right at the first intersection they encountered, and walked past a staircase identical to the flight of steps by the building's entrance-way. As they wandered down the gloomy hallway, icy air enveloped them. A cold wind was blowing through a double-wide doorway at the end of the hall, a vestibule that led into a room much more massive than the one they had just ventured through.

The two shaggy men walked under a sign that read "Chow Hall" and into a high-ceilinged chamber crammed full of long tables, both freezing in their tracks the moment they entered. The northern wall of the room had been caved in from the outside; chilly air was pouring in through the twenty-foot-wide aperture, over the colossal remains of a slain Pale Giant. The dead creature was face-down on the floor of the Chow Hall, its body nothing more than a skeleton whose flesh had decayed over many years. The Giant's skin was paper-thin and pocked with countless bullet holes.

A violent crashing noise suddenly reverberated through the wall to Jonah's left, near a sign that read "Kitchen." The crashing was followed by muted hissing and sounds of strange words being spoken in an unknown language. Jonah clicked the flashlight off, grabbed Barry by the arm, and rushed along the wall. They scurried down the last row of tables into the far corner of the room and crouched behind a table bench. Gasping for air, Jonah nervously peered over the table at the kitchen door.

"Is it the guards?" Barry squeaked, helpless panic rising in his chest.

"I don't know," Jonah admitted, and gulped.

They endured motionless silence for an endless period, waiting for something to happen. When the kitchen door was suddenly kicked open and two scaly creatures with red, glowing eyes emerged,

Jonah almost wet his pants. The young Masters were each carrying two steel pots, one of which was filled with kitchen utensils. Their snouts spouted steam as they crept through a maze of knocked-over tables, heading for the caved-in wall.

The taller of the two creatures began yelling at the other in a series of hisses and snarls. Its long fangs chomped and expunged spittle as it admonished the shorter one, who replied with equally violent sounds.

"Sssspeak human," the taller Master abruptly spat in growling English.

"Patsss and pansss," the smaller one said awkwardly.

"Potsss and pansss, for ssssale," it corrected, and powerfully shoved a table aside, clearing a path for both of them.

"Potsss and pansss, for ssssale," the other repeated.

Jonah started to feel tremors in the bench he was leaning against; he turned and found Barry right next to him, staring at the hideous creatures. Barry was shaking uncontrollably, his eyes wide with oncoming madness. "Don't look anymore," he whispered. Barry nodded and turned away, dropping to his knees.

As Barry crawled toward the wall, his foot accidentally nudged an empty can, sending it rolling over the floor. The reverberating noise made the two Masters halt immediately in their tracks and suspend their conversation. Jonah quickly ducked down, taking care to get as flat as possible against the floor without making a sound. Barry rolled to his side and gently fell to the floor, where he curled into the fetal position. Jonah could hear the two monsters sniffing the air.

"Flavored humanssss, not ssssuppossssed to be here, like ussss. Ssssmellssss like… broccoli and beef," one hissed in between snorts of breath, "very expenssssive tasssste."

"We cannot eat here," the other creature growled. The bitter-sounding statement was followed by a period of silent deliberation. "Name thissss," it suddenly said, with a smile in its terrifying voice. The sound of metal clinking against metal echoed in the distance.

"Sssspoon, for ssssale," the other replied.

An object whizzed over the table that Jonah and Barry were hiding behind and ricocheted off the wall. It fell to the floor with a noisy clang, less than a foot from Jonah's face. The sturdy steel cooking spoon had been twisted into a "V."

"Wassste," one Master reprimanded the other.

Sounds of shuffling feet signaled that the creatures were walking away. Not trusting his ears, Jonah pushed himself up to his knees and gazed over the rows of tables to gather reconnaissance. He watched the two Masters haul their looted treasures over a mound of concrete rubble and then jump through the opening of the caved-in wall, finally disappearing into the cold night air.

After a few seconds, Jonah found his voice. "That was way too close, and there could be more of them in there," he said, eyeing the kitchen. "They could smell us, our assigned foods!" he said in an indignant, loud whisper. Barry's mind was too numb to hear Jonah. He forced himself off the floor and sat delicately on the table bench, where he could gather his wits.

Jonah stood up and parked his hands on his hips. "We haven't found any more food or water down here, and I'm afraid to go look in that room," he said as he eyed the kitchen door. "Let's go back up, far away from here, and start again."

Jonah offered his hand to Barry; the thin, scruffy former inmate eventually accepted it and forced himself to stand up. As they retraced their steps back to the hallway, Barry's knees were still a little shaky, but the shock and fright of the previous few minutes was gradually wearing off. They stealthily hurried out of the Chow Hall and up the nearest set of stairs, neither man wanting to discuss their close brush with death.

Jonah knew they couldn't stay there now, not unless they barricaded themselves in a room until they died, just like female 19.

* * *

6:58 P.M.

As they searched the second floor of the enormous decaying building, every sound made them jump. Exploring wordlessly, they inspected each room for supplies and came up empty. They ascended the creaky staircase, hoping a miracle was somewhere to be found on the fourth floor. Jonah was grateful that they had some sort of shelter, even with what happened in the Chow Hall. Chancing it out in the forest with the animals was suicide, and night was already upon them. Tonight, they would have to pick a room as far from the Chow Hall as possible, pile furniture against the door, and hope for the best.

After they reached the top, Jonah and Barry found an odd small metal room situated next to the staircase, a feature that was only on the fourth floor. Jonah poked his head inside the room and found a group of buttons that were numbered 1 to 4.

Barry looked down both of the long hallways skeptically; Jonah could almost see smoke coming out of his ears as his mind labored through the fifty-fifty decision. "Let's have some pills," Jonah proclaimed, knowing that the words would put his friend at ease. He unsealed the near-empty bag that once held a mighty hoard and gave Barry two red and two orange, then counted out the same for himself. He shook the bag, searching for orange and red pills.

"These are the last orange pills, except the old ones," he said, doing his best to sound nonchalant. "We have three red left."

Barry chose to ignore the frightening information. He tossed the pills in his mouth, washed them down with the last of his water, and burped. He dropped the empty plastic bottle down the stairs, where it fell end over end and bounced against a pile of rubble on the lower landing. "I'm sorry about earlier, making the noise and all. It was an accident."

"They didn't kill us, so it doesn't matter." Jonah swallowed his pills and resealed the bag, thinking through their investigation options. One direction led to the far reaches of the building, an area three floors above the Chow Hall; the other to a set of rooms above the entranceway and the File Room. They needed to find a place to sleep for the night, and he refused to stay in the same room as female 19.

"This way." Jonah followed his instincts and trudged off to the right, avoiding the other end of the top floor until that was the only place left to look.

Rooms on both sides of the hallway matched the appearance of those on the other floors, but as they got farther through the fourth level, they found the size of each room increasing, as was the volume of trash on the floor. Peculiar symbols began to appear above the doorways, and they weren't letters or numbers, although one of them did look like two 1's standing side by side. They stopped in front of the symbol and stared, confused over what it could mean. Barry reached up and tried to pry the symbol off the concrete above the doorway with long, dirty fingernails, but the two interconnected vertical silver bars wouldn't budge. Jonah scanned through the other symbols, finding many different kinds of markings. He pointed the flashlight at the far end of the hall, to a room one story directly above the File Room. Three glittering five-pointed stars were centered above the doorway.

"Those are stars, like we talked about in class." Jonah had been fascinated by stars since the moment he learned about them. The shape of the stars above the doorway was identical to what Headmaster Green had drawn on the chalkboard.

They walked past the rooms that preceded the stars and carefully looked in each, discovering only the usual: wet papers; crumbling drywall; and shabby, water-damaged furniture. As they crept toward the last of the unsearched rooms, the dimming flashlight beam revealed something disturbing on the floor. A plate-sized splatter of dried blood stained the wood directly under the three silver stars. Hanging from the door was a broken lock and a bloodstained hasp; a large chunk of concrete was on the ground nearby. It seemed as though someone had broken into the room by smashing the lock with the concrete and had been injured in the process.

Barry pushed on the door with two fingers, and it slowly swung open. The two men entered a grand, luxurious suite of polished furnishings and plush carpet, and were immediately overwhelmed by what they saw. Chairs and tables were neatly arranged, blankets covering beds were tucked in, and framed pictures hung unbroken on the walls. To the two former prisoners of Cydonia 6, it was the most beautiful place on Earth.

Jonah wandered through the darkened suite, a lavish sensation cushioning each step, his head swiveling in sync with the meandering flashlight beam. The living quarters had the look, smell, and feel of abandonment. Dust was layered on the furniture like snow; he dragged his middle finger across the top of a dresser as he passed, revealing polished wood. They hadn't come across any other rooms as beautiful, and as preserved, as this. Another difference between this chamber and the others (except the File Room) was that the suite didn't have any windows. Jonah shook his head, not understanding. Even his cell back in camp had a window.

Jonah and Barry worked their way toward the recesses of the living quarters, a space full of comfortable-looking chairs, a hefty wooden desk, and a bar adorned with crystal bottles and glasses. This section of the luxurious quarters resembled Headmaster Green's office, but it was much more spacious and filled with high-quality furnishings.

The flashlight beam came across a river of empty cans and plastic water bottles that led to a half-closed closet door. The cans and bottles looked identical to those they had found next to female 19. Seeing the cans and bottles simultaneously, Jonah and Barry clamored for the closet door, kicking away debris as they opened it.

Inside the closet were stacks of corrugated boxes, with one empty box lying ripped open on the floor. They each dove into a box, collecting an armful of supplies.

"It's full!" Barry shrieked with excitement. "There's a bunch in here!"

"I know, I know! We should have looked here first!" Jonah furiously grabbed water bottles and cans, heaping them together in his arms.

Unable to carry anything else, the men stumbled out of the closet and into the office, where they dumped the supplies onto the middle section of a long couch. Jonah and Barry flopped down on both sides of the pile of cans and bottles and dug in. Although the cushions were missing from the couch, it still made a fine resting place.

"Read this!" Barry shoved a can of food into Jonah's face.

Jonah didn't recognize the word written across it, but he also knew what the word wasn't. "Not beef." Barry pried the can open and scooped out brown chunks. Jonah found a can of beef-flavored dog food and followed suit. They ate and drank as much as they wanted, knowing that a stack of boxes still remained in the closet.

His stomach now bulging with food, Jonah ran his index finger around the rim of his third can and smeared what he gathered onto his tongue. He sat back, relaxing, his eyes drifting to a row of frames hanging high on the wall behind the desk. He cast the flashlight beam on a flag that had been folded into a triangle, then moved the light to a row of colorful medals; next to the medals was a paper calendar that showed a date of December 2297 M.E. Small writing covered some of the boxes on the calendar, including the last box, December 57th, where three bold black words were written: "New Year's Party."

He moved the light to his right and stopped on a long piece of paper that was crammed with neatly arranged words of varying sizes. He could clearly see the largest of the words, which were written in big block letters across the top portion of the rectangular paper, but he didn't know what they meant. Jonah got to his feet and circled around the desk as Barry popped open a fresh can of dog food. He walked over to the framed newspaper and studied the headline, which read, "Humans Colonize Mars."

Above the block letters was more large writing, a logo that named the time-faded publication the *Global Conglomerate News*. Again, Jonah couldn't comprehend the stylistically shaped letters, but they looked interesting. The significance of the newspaper's date—February 25, 2199—was also lost on him.

He walked along the wall, moving the light from frame to frame, studying the headlines for recognizable words. "Blue Skies on the Red Planet" was splashed across the top of another newspaper; this time, the publication logo had been shortened to *GCN*, and it was dated June 22, 2259. The bottom portion of the paper contained the sub-headline "Martian Terraform Reaches Final Phase."

Barry pushed himself up from the couch and threw his empty can into the pile by the closet. He strolled along the wall, picking his teeth with his fingernail, and came up behind Jonah, who was perusing the many rows of words stacked across the framed newspaper. "Shit, that's a lot of writing," Barry said, and yawned. Jonah grunted, the comment bouncing off. "What does it all say?"

"It's about Mars. Headmaster Green said Mars is a planet, like the moon, remember?" Jonah suggested hopefully.

Barry shook his head. "No. Did Columbus go there too?"

"How would I know?" Jonah said dismissively. He nodded toward the newspaper. "This has words about people living on Mars."

Barry walked past Jonah and squinted closely at the next framed newspaper, which was smaller than the *GCN*. "This one looks different than that one," he said, pointing to the newspaper, unable to discern a single word.

Jonah moved alongside him and turned the light on the publication logo, revealing the words *Aries Chronicle*. Four headlines written in bold ink divided the front page into quarters; from the top going clockwise, they read, "Intelligent Life on Mars," "Earth Shuttles to Double," "Calculating Martian Time," and finally, "Pyramids Mapped in Cydonia Zone."

Jonah pointed to the last headline. "That says Cydonia, just like on the Cydonia 6 sign in the yard."

Barry nodded, pretending to understand the significance of the word. He had never thought of reading the signs in the yard, much less remembering what the words looked like. Right now, he couldn't picture the yard. It was somehow distant and vague in his memory. They had been out for only a day and a half, but it already felt like years.

Jonah rubbed his beard. "Cydonia Zone," he said to himself.

"Like gray zone," Barry blurted, hoping it would help. "This looks crazy," he said, pointing to a grid of numbers under the "Calculating Martian Time" headline, a table of equations that converted Earth years, days, hours, and minutes into their corresponding Martian Era (M.E.) values. Barry's finger dragged across a line of mysterious symbols and words that read, "687 day year = 1.88 Earth years"; he stared at Jonah, his brow raised hopefully.

Jonah rolled his eyes at the numbers, immediately giving up on trying to interpret their meaning. "I don't know what it means!" He turned and squinted at the last framed newspaper, which had been smashed. Shards of glass and shredded paper were scattered on the floor below the broken frame. He didn't want to risk walking on the sharp slivers of glass that littered the carpet and was thoroughly bored with the process of reading.

"What do you want to do now?" Jonah said, and stretched his back.

"We could sleep," Barry suggested hopefully.

Conflicted, Jonah leaned back on the large desk and pushed himself up, sitting on it.

"What's the matter?"

Jonah rubbed his face and then folded his hands in his lap. "We can't stay here like she did. Not with the monsters and the hole in the wall. Eventually, we need to find somewhere else to go."

Barry walked over to the wide desk and hopped on, sitting next to Jonah. He swung his feet as he considered options. "We could follow the black line again tomorrow, see where it goes; take a bunch of food and water with us," he added.

"What do you think we'll find out there, another camp? A place like this but with people?" Jonah knew they would be—yet again—walking into a mysterious and risky future if they left. At least here they had a roof over their heads and relative protection from hostile elements, particularly monsters and animals, as long as they stayed hidden.

"There has to be other stuff," Barry encouraged. "Dr. Selleck said he came from a place called City."

Jonah considered what could be waiting for them in the forest and beyond, and shivered. "Let's sleep on it and talk tomorrow."

CHAPTER 23

Carter and Blake had left Fort Martius with a platoon of soldiers less than forty minutes ago. Upon arrival at the main gate of Fort Garvey, an abandoned facility on the outer rim of the border, the soldiers had split up into six patrols and began searching the grounds in a grid. Since Blake was the senior non-commissioned officer in the platoon, he drew the most dangerous duty. Something alive was on the fourth floor of the main building; his job was to find out what it was.

Carter nervously checked the small computer screen strapped to her arm for a data update as she hurried up the staircase behind Blake. She quickly returned her focus to the sight on the end of her machine-gun barrel, knowing that organic imaging technology was helpful but not foolproof. Sensor errors were rare, but it was even rarer for sensors to scan unregistered serial numbers out in the middle of nowhere.

"Checking north," Blake said quietly into his com-link, as he veered right at the top of the staircase, the small flashlight attached to his rifle barrel steadily illuminating the hallway and darkened doorways ahead.

Carter was happy to have a vet like Blake as a partner, especially tonight. He had the highest kill count of the entire battalion. But Blake hadn't expressed an equal share of confidence in being paired with a rookie, and she couldn't blame him. Combat was a concept she knew only from training, and a video screen couldn't kill you like a fifty-ton, bloodthirsty IIL could.

Stories had been circling the base for the past two weeks about a squad of six soldiers who went out into uncharted territory to locate a group of missing miners. Instead of miners, the soldiers found the Pale Giant that ate them; the miners' sensors were still being digested inside the IIL's four stomachs as the team fought, and eventually killed, the colossal creature. Four of the six soldiers died on the spot; a fifth died in surgery back on base.

Carter followed protocol and sporadically checked their flank, not wanting to be taken by surprise. The IILs that talked, the ones that named themselves the Masters, were fiendishly clever and notoriously hard to kill. The Giants, she heard through rumors, couldn't be taken down with anything less than explosives.

Blake stopped in front of the door of the former quarters of General Garvey, the legendary wartime strategist who had brought an end to the bloodiest conflict in human history. He pointed his rifle at the floor, indicating a dried splatter of blood that looked years old. He nodded to Carter; she slung her rifle and typed into the screen on her arm, keying in a code that would prepare backup for mobilization. She set her gun back into the crook of her shoulder and nodded to Blake, indicating readiness to proceed. All it took now was pressing a button and the thirty-nine other soldiers in their platoon would be on them in less than a minute.

Blake tried to push the door open, but it was stuck. He lowered his rifle, leaned into the door with his shoulder, and gradually worked it open. Someone, or something, had blocked the door with a living room chair; Blake created enough room for them to squeeze through, then immediately fit the butt of his rifle back into his shoulder. They entered quickly and silently, guns up, ready for anything. The sound of two loud voices drew them quickly to the General's office. Blake entered first, Carter two steps behind him.

Two thin, dirty men with long hair and scruffy beards were standing by the General's desk, each wearing a long-sleeved burlap shirt and tattered burlap pants. One had a patch with the number 23 on the left breast of his shirt; the other wore number 24.

Jonah dropped the clean blanket he had been stretching out over the floor, frozen in terror. The guards had found them.

Carter circled to the right as Blake stayed in position. She noticed that neither man was wearing shoes. A plastic bag of pills was lying on the desk, and cans and plastic water bottles were scattered across a nearby couch.

"Who are you?" Blake demanded; his rifle remained trained on Jonah's forehead.

Petrified, neither man answered immediately. "Male 24," Jonah eventually squeaked; he recognized one of the two guards as being female and didn't want to risk saying his name.

"Male 23," Barry said quickly.

"Names." Carter was relieved but very confused.

"Are we allowed to say?" the one wearing 23 said to Blake.

"Drop the weapon." Blake's eyes flicked to the flashlight in Barry's right hand. Barry dropped the water bottle he was holding in his left hand.

"The flashlight!" Carter spat. She could tell that the two strange-looking men were intimidated, but that didn't mean they weren't a threat. Barry dropped the flashlight and shimmied closer to Jonah, huddling beside him.

Blake and Carter exchanged glances, silently agreeing that the two men were not hostile, and lowered their rifles. "I'm Sergeant Blake; this is Private Carter, border security. Who are you?"

"Jonah and Barry," Jonah said nervously as he pointed to himself and then to his friend. "My food is… was broccoli." He hoped the gesture of sharing what food he had been assigned would break the tension.

Instead, Blake's face wrinkled up. "So what?"

"Let's see IDs," Carter ordered, but the two disheveled men obviously had no idea what she meant. Their baffled eyes searched internally for a translation.

"What's IDs?" Barry asked innocently.

Jonah picked up a can from the couch and offered it to Carter. "Is this your food? We ate some and drank the water."

Carter kept her eyes on Jonah as she accepted the can. She slowly stepped back and turned the can in her hand. "This is dog food."

"We were hungry," Barry said meekly, fear lingering in his belly.

"How did you get here?" Blake asked sharply.

"Through the excretion duct, in the marriage hut." To Jonah, the explanation made perfect sense, but instead it perplexed Blake even more.

"Before that, where were you?"

"Cydonia 6." Jonah regretted the admission but felt he had to answer honestly.

"You escaped from a Cydonia camp and *walked* here?" Carter challenged in disbelief. Jonah and Barry nodded. "Is anyone else here?"

"Female 19. But she's dead," Jonah amended quickly.

"How did she die?" Carter was more curious than concerned.

"She escaped before us, a long time ago. We just found her," Barry said defensively.

Blake released a long breath as he took off his helmet and ran his fingers through his sweaty hair. He slowly walked to a nearby chair and sat down heavily. After much deliberation, he leaned forward and turned to Carter. "I'll call it in; you get their statement."

"Whatever you think is best," Carter said, slightly befuddled by his behavior.

Blake got up from the chair and exited the office as he typed into the screen attached to his forearm. They both knew the report he was about to convey was a doozy, but Carter had no idea of the PR nightmare they were about to be entangled in.

"Patrol 5, report," Carter heard Blake say as he walked down the hall and through the kitchen.

"Go ahead," a garbled voice replied, as Jonah and Barry curiously listened to the exchange.

"Found two escaped zone products in sector Delta, fourth floor."

"Say again?" the crackling, distant voice answered.

"We found two zone products. No, this is not a joke; they were just…" Blake's voice faded as he walked out of the suite and closed the door behind him.

"Who else is here?" Jonah's voice shook.

"That's his com-link. There's other soldiers outside, on the floors below us, some on the road too." Carter walked closer, examining them. The one wearing 24 had bloodstains all over his shirt. "Are you injured?" She realized the question wasn't sinking in. "Are you hurt?"

Barry shook his head; Jonah was distracted by something. "What's 'zone' mean, Carter?" Jonah asked carefully.

"Cydonia Zone—it's a big piece of land to the east, where you two came from. Ancestors of the IILs built pyramids there millions of years ago. It's kind of like their version of Jerusalem, a holy land. Fort Garvey, this place, is right on the border of the Cydonia Zone." She pointed to the ground to emphasize her meaning. "We're just inside human territory."

"We saw two monsters in a room on the ground. They saw us too but didn't kill us," Jonah found himself babbling, but Carter was listening carefully.

"When did you see them, where did you see them, and what were they doing?" she asked, suddenly alert.

"A while ago," Jonah said, hesitating, unsure of how to quantify the time of their encounter with the monsters. "It was a big room with tables, and they were taking pots and spoons away," Jonah said, making sure to recall as much information as possible.

"You're sure you only saw two of them?" she asked sharply.

Jonah nodded confidently. "Yeah, one tall, and one short. They wanted to eat us."

Carter slowly relaxed. "Probably just scavengers; sometimes they sneak across the border and steal what they can carry. But they would never kill or eat you inside human territory—it would be really bad for business," she reassured.

Carter heard the door open and quickly pointed her rifle back toward the hallway. "It's me," Blake said distantly.

She lowered her gun as Blake strode back into the room. "They saw two Masters, somewhere on the ground floor."

"Scavengers, you think?" Blake asked curiously.

"We saw *monsters*, not masters," Jonah interjected, wanting to participate in the conversation. It was his story to tell, anyway. "They had pots and pans, and said we smelled like broccoli and beef."

Blake smiled, mostly from Jonah's naïveté, and turned to Carter. "We're pulling out; meet them back on the road."

She nodded, happy to hear it. Although they were minutes away from wrapping up, she wouldn't be able to fully relax until they drove through the gate back at the base. She turned back to the two skinny men, but something on the floor, glinting off the flashlight beam, caught her eye. She walked over to a smashed picture frame that was hanging on the wall and found a tattered newspaper. Glass crunched under her boots as she raised the flaps of the torn paper and pressed it against the wall so she could read it.

Carter recognized the newspaper immediately, specifically the famous picture, and an even more famous headline that was splashed across the front page. She unpinned the tattered paper from the frame and folded it in half.

Blake stood two paces from Jonah and Barry, hesitating to speak as he mulled over questions. "The chief wants to know how many are left back at your camp, inmates and staff. Do you know?"

"None," Barry said quickly.

"They're all dead?"

"Yes," Jonah sheepishly admitted. He hoped that Blake didn't want details.

"Do you know why you were there?"

Blake's directness surprised Carter, who walked back to the group of men, holding the folded newspaper. She wanted to hear the answer too. Most people didn't know about the Cydonia camps and what they were, but the GCMC certainly did. The camps were the reason why the war ended and a lot of human lives were spared.

"So monsters could eat us," Jonah said flatly.

"You're payments, products… bribes that keep the monsters from eating the rest of us."

Carter was afraid to see the effect of the information take hold on the former inmates, but they clearly hadn't absorbed the explanation all the way. She unfolded the tattered newspaper, showing it to Jonah and Barry, and pointed to a picture of a smiling man in a military uniform who was shaking hands with an eight-foot-tall, scaly monster with spear-like fangs and a pudgy snout for a nose. "This is General Garvey; you're standing in his old office," Carter said, as if teaching a classroom of young children.

"That's what we saw, monsters." Jonah pointed to the tall, horrific-looking creature in the photo. It resembled the two creatures in the Chow Hall and the one they had narrowly escaped in the tunnels below camp.

"They refer to themselves as Masters; they don't really use names," Blake explained coolly. "It's sort of an ego thing—making sure that humans remember who the dominant species is here."

"What do all these words say?" Barry blurted awkwardly, ignoring everything he had just heard. "And why is it shaking hands with the man?"

Jonah rolled his eyes, embarrassed by Barry's illiteracy. It was true, Jonah couldn't read all of the words, even the one word written in big block letters that took up the top third of the torn newspaper, but he wouldn't admit it to strangers so openly.

Carter pointed to the headline. "This says 'TRUCE.' There was a long war, where humans fought the IILs for control of this planet. Lots of people were killed; a lot of work was ruined. The truce ended the war.

"This is General Garvey shaking hands with a Master, the same day the truce was signed, on April 3, 2309, Martian Era." Carter tapped the date of the newspaper with her finger and studied the two ragged skeletons standing before her, skeptical that they grasped what was being said to them. The one wearing number 24 looked exponentially more confused than the other one. She had already forgotten their names.

"What's IILs?" Jonah finally asked as gears turned in his head. Carter's story, and the picture in particular, were making certain memories and thoughts connect. Hilda fought in a war, so did the Headmaster, but he never knew the war was fought over control of the Earth.

"Indigenous Intelligent Lifeforms," she said, and then quickly backtracked. "These things." She pointed to the newspaper, and the picture of the Master. "There's other ones too, but whatever; for now, it means this," she said, tapping the photo.

"I'm getting a picture," Blake announced, and held his forearm up, tilting the screen toward the two shaggy men. When the flash went off, Barry and Jonah blinked rapidly, dazzled by the sudden burst of light.

Carter smirked, knowing that the image, and a funny caption, would soon appear on the GCMC's Chrono-Proxy feed. Everyone with access to the network, including past and future users, should get a good laugh out of this one.

"Patrol 5?" Blake's com-link loudly blared, making all four of them jump.

"Go ahead," he replied as he adjusted the com-link's speaker volume.

"We're Oscar Mike, over," the speaker crackled, the word making both soldiers perk up.

"OK, let's go," Blake waved at the door with his rifle, urging Jonah and Barry to file out.

"Don't take us back," Jonah pleaded fearfully, tears suddenly welling in his eyes.

"We won't, I promise. Laws prevent us from sending you back," Blake said reassuringly. "You're free men now."

"We're taking you to our base, a big place full of soldiers, where it's safe," Carter clarified. "You give a statement, then get some money and a ticket back to Terra. It's all part of a settlement package for former prisoners. You're not the first ones to have escaped."

"It'll all be explained," Blake nodded, hoping the questions would end.

"What's... where's Terra? A place like this?" Jonah pointed to the ground.

"Earth," Carter said bluntly.

Stunned, Jonah's eyes widened and his jaw dropped. The words he wanted to say suddenly froze in the back of his throat.

"Where are... we now?" Barry stammered.

"Mars." Carter was confused; she didn't know what the big deal was. "Terraform's been going on a couple hundred years now."

"Mars? But that's... we're..." Jonah suddenly felt light-headed, and the room began to spin. As Carter's face transformed into a blurry smear, he crashed to the floor.

Blake breathed out, annoyed. He didn't want to have to carry the stinking man down to the transport, regardless of how thin he was.

Barry, unfazed, looked down at Jonah's unconscious body and then turned to Blake. "Do you have any orange pills?"

CHAPTER 0

The Cydonia murder camps became active less than a year after the century-long, interspecies war ended. Some say the conflict began because humans had been encroaching on the IILs' sacred territory, a seemingly arbitrary quantity of land and (newly restored) ocean that became known as the Cydonia Zone. But the truth is, no one really knows why the horrific, enigmatic creatures suddenly started killing everyone. What is known, however, is why they stopped.

On April 59th of the year 2309 M.E., General Thurgood Garvey ordered GCMC 1st Battalion into the center of the Cydonia Zone to administer and defend construction of the first two camps. In four months, both facilities were stocked and secured, and then the process of product flavor infusions began. Certain members of the press called it a deal with devils, but to General Garvey and the Governor, it was a necessary, welcomed arrangement. The humans were on the brink of losing the war and being exterminated. But if everything went as planned, there would be peace, and the public would receive almost no information about the camps once they were opened.

Cydonia 1 and Cydonia 2 were designed by the IILs that called themselves the Masters, a genus of violent and hideously ugly organisms that would come to live beneath two very unusual restaurants. The Masters micromanaged every construction detail of these customized, assembly-line killing facilities, issuing orders and revising product flavor specifications from the darkened sewers beneath the camps.

A vast subterranean hive of tunnels linked the sewers under Cydonia 1 and 2 to the Masters' stronghold, a seven-sided pyramid so ancient and so colossal that it blended into the mountain range that surrounded it. For decades, humans simply mistook the heptagonal edifice for a mountain. When the true nature of the prehistoric structure was finally revealed, mankind was faced with an inexplicable reality: they were not the only intelligent organisms on the planet. Indigenous Intelligent Lifeforms (since shortened to the military code IIL) had been there all along.

During the first wave of IIL night attacks in 2207 M.E., hordes of bloodthirsty monsters would ambush a colony; slaughter hundreds (sometimes thousands) of men, women, and children; and then vanish before sunrise. Survivors told stories of tall, scaly pigs that stood on two legs, with sharp fangs and spear-length claws. The deformed, red-eyed creatures ate their kills in the aftermath of an attack and could somehow *speak in English*.

Humans studied the pattern of assaults and found that they had all occurred within a two hundred–mile radius of a particular mountain range. Sub-orbital surveying cameras scanned the grid and zeroed in on an anomaly approximately seventy-five million square feet in size. Most of the seven-sided pyramid was buried, with less than a quarter exposed to the elements; all remotely conducted tests confirmed that it had been artificially constructed, in the late Hesperian Period, more than three billion years before their cameras came across it.

The Masters proved to be exceptionally intelligent and possessed uncannily powerful senses, especially those of smell and taste. As the first attack wave withdrew, the Masters retrieved printed records, writings, and photographs from their human victims, and brought the materials back to their pyramid, where they studied their enemy. Within days, they could speak and write in every known language; concepts and culture of those living above ground had been absorbed almost instantly. Among the mélange of publications that had been taken from human settlements were cookbooks, a happenstance that would change the course of history.

The Masters were increasingly exposed to the exterior world as decades passed in the war between species. Their libraries of confiscated books and papers expanded, as did their knowledge of their adversary. As a result, the Masters developed an unexpected fascination with human cooking, particularly the process of combining foods to create different flavors. They never knew that such a variety of treats to their primary two senses existed. And once the urge to experience luxurious and exotic tastes was indulged, it was too strong for them to suppress.

While attacks expanded across the globe, the Masters sought out and hoarded cookbooks as war prizes, and raided the chow halls of conquered military bases for spices and cooking equipment. Their interest in aromas and tastes had metastasized into an obsession, and ended up being the primary reason for the cessation of hostilities.

At first the Masters tried eating the same food as humans did, but their digestive systems didn't get along well with traditionally cooked meats and vegetables. After some tinkering, they arrived at a uniquely macabre way to fulfill their epicurean impulses without having to suffer through intestinal pain. Humans would eat the food, and the Masters would eat the humans.

Flavor-infusion protocol at the Cydonia murder camps was a cruel but effective process. Human products would be force-fed one food for virtually their entire lives, so their flesh would smell and taste like that food. To speed things along, growth hormones would be injected into the products, making them age faster and quickening muscle growth. Since the Masters had been eating raw human flesh for a hundred years, the solution was the simplest way to comfortably satiate their bizarre cravings.

The Masters proposed that if General Garvey and his Global Conglomerate overseers built the prison camps, filled the flavor orders, and followed the rules, they could keep three quarters of the planet and the attacks would stop. The remaining quarter of the planet, the Cydonia Zone, would then be recognized as a sovereign nation controlled solely by the IILs—the Masters and their even more obscure allies, the Pale Giants.

Unlike the Masters, the rarely seen Giants roamed free among the mountains and forests of the Cydonia Zone, had no known language, and survived the prewar period on subterranean plants and fungus. After air quality stabilized in the first half of the twenty-second century, the enormous humanoids left their caverns and tunnels and began inhabiting the surrounding forests, being active only at night. They rapidly adapted to fresh air and the elements, and evolved into omnivores, soon cultivating a taste for humans that would rival the Masters', but in a more rudimentary way.

The Giants' new taste for flesh initially came at the expense of pioneers and livestock, but as the war dragged on, they began hunting colonists and soldiers. Whenever the Giants attacked, they killed everything in sight. It was the tales of explorers that gave a name to these nocturnal, albino behemoths, the Pale Giants, as nothing else could more succinctly describe them.

The Giants and the Masters had fought alongside each other as tenuous allies during the century-long conflict with the humans. Somehow, they maintained a friendly, yet competitive, cohabitation of the same territory after the war.

As peace continued through the postwar period, new camps started popping up in the Cydonia Zone. The Masters were now paying in gold for the services of the human camp administrators. Profits were secretly funneled into the colonies through the government, kickbacks were made, and interspecies business between the Masters and the humans became a shadow industry.

Cydonia 1 and 2 were the largest camps, each holding twenty

inmates, and were located so far inside IIL territory that they could operate without interference from the colonies. Products were separated by sex, with males interned in Cydonia 1 and females in Cydonia 2. Lot liquidation was quick, with replacements frequently trucked in from the transition camp, a holding facility for unallocated and undeveloped inventory.

Camps 3–12 were spread across the vast territory of the Cydonia Zone, each constructed within reasonable transport distance from human territory, and housed both men and women. The Masters managing the new locations were patient and demanded more flavor complexity in the products. Lot liquidation, as a result, grew into a prolonged process that required more involvement from the human staff. At one time, the sixth Cydonia camp was the strategic headquarters for Global Conglomerate Marine Corps (GCMC) Western Command.

* * *

At one time, the sixth Cydonia camp was the strategic headquarters for Global Conglomerate Marine Corps (GCMC) Western Command. The base, like everything else in IIL territory, was forfeited by the humans in the Truce of Cydonia. The GCMC added four guard towers and a thirty-foot-high fence to the facility, creating the holding area for the products to be housed there, and then began withdrawal of forces. The fence and towers had been hastily thrown together and sloppily erected in the wake of evacuation, but they would endure for decades.

Until, that is, everything was ripped down by the IILs in the year 2335 M.E.

Initially, the facility was defended by a garrison of twenty soldiers, a unit of combat veterans who were assigned to protect inmates and staff from the IILs that inhabited the forest that surrounded the camp. When the second lot of products arrived, the military presence was reduced by half, leaving only ten men and women on full-time duty. After the second group of prisoners were sent to their death, the remaining soldiers were recalled to human territory, and day-to-day control of Cydonia 6 was turned over to the four civilian staff members.

By the time the last lot of human products was trucked into Cydonia 6, the guard towers were dilapidated and diseased from neglect and the passage of time. The thirty-foot-high chain fence that connected the four towers drooped in sections; the barbed wire topping the fence was missing on the west section and was unraveling in other areas. But to those held captive within it, the fence was impregnable; it surrounded everything they would ever know about the world and protected them from the dangers that lay beyond its borders.

The prisoners' repetitive existence revolved around eating assigned foods. Four times a day, every day, the same organic material was served and consumed. Their strict diet was supplemented by narcotics, steroids, and growth hormones; exercise was limited solely to walking in the yard.

The yard was the inmates' preferred setting for social interaction, as it was the only place they could talk about whatever they wanted to as a group. At different intervals, the male inmates and female inmates could wander the length of the splotchy, yellowish-green field of grass, as long as they didn't cross a demarcation known as the Lines of Division.

The Lines were two wide strips of black and white plastic that bisected the yard into equal halves, with a black strip setting the boundary for the men's side, and a white strip for the women's. Only an inch in height and three feet in breadth, the parallel lines traveled all the way from the middle of the north fence to the south fence. The Lines were secured flatly to the ground with heavy iron stakes; even during the worst storms, the plastic divider would never move. The border kept the sexes apart and inmates controlled. Crossing the Lines would result in an unimaginable penalty, so males and females never physically interacted.

Structures and features of the camp were mirrored on either side of the Lines of Division. Two one-story buildings made of cheap, mottled wood served as the men's and women's barracks, with the men occupying the western half of the yard and the women the eastern half.

The shoddily built, flat-roofed huts each held five inmates; the wall of the hut that faced the Lines of Division had three windows, all of which were covered with grids of rebar. The entrance to the barracks was in the back of the building, in the middle of the wall facing the exterior fence. The two inmate windows on the side overlooking the fence were also covered with rusty rebar.

Sturdy shutters made of thick, pressure-treated wooden panels covered the inmates' windows every night, each attached to the barracks wall with steel bolts. Oddly, shutters could be properly secured only from the *inside* of an inmate's cell; unknown to them, it was a measure taken for their protection.

Shutters were a very important part of camp routine; they had to be opened every morning and closed every evening. Prisoners were told that having your window open at night was against the rules and punishable by death, the implied threat being that the camp's staff would execute them. In reality, it meant the inmates would be slaughtered by the IILs.

Within the yard, on either side of the Lines of Division near the south fence gates, were two large, door-size planks of warped wood that served as coverings for two crudely fashioned ditches. It was here, at what was known as the hole, that inmates were isolated from the others for unusually bad behavior. The inmate being punished would first be tranquilized and then thrown in the hole. The wooden plank would slide over the ditch; then a heavy stone would be placed on top of the plank, pinning the wood to the ground. By the time the stone was rolled into place, the inmate inside the grave-sized ditch would already be unconscious.

Adjacent to the yard, the hole, and the inmates' barracks was the administration area, a separately secured grouping of small buildings that shared the south fence with the yard. This was the only region of camp that male and female inmates both accessed, but never at the same time. The sturdily constructed ex-military base was the mirror opposite of the yard; it was surrounded by fortified fencing, and each building inside the area (except for one) was made of blast-proof concrete.

The lone exception was the marriage hut, a double-wide cell outfitted with shutters and rebar-covered windows that was modeled on the layout of the inmates' barracks. The hut was a stark visual contrast to the durable buildings surrounding its walls. The small, cheaply crafted edifice resembled an oversized toolshed and was rarely used.

Cydonia 6's fourth lot, numbered 20–24, was an ordinary sampling of human products—their minds naïve and uneducated, their bodies supple with lean muscle. For the most part, the inmates' behavior was mild, and they conformed to camp rules. But as the prisoners matured and hormones developed, love somehow got in the way.

The End